THE SILVERSMITH

DAVID WOLF BOOK 2

JEFF CARSON

CROSS ATLANTIC PUBLISHING

Add Audible Narration Instantly

Click Here to ADD AUDIBLE NARRATION of THE SILVERSMITH, narrated by Sean Patrick Hopkins.

CHAPTER 1

SERGEANT DAVID WOLF leaned against the bumper of his Sluice County Sheriff's Department-issue Ford Explorer and watched a few angry people stream out of the town hall building.

It was warm already for a September morning and getting hotter by the second, and Wolf was sweating under his khaki uniform shirt.

"Oh my God," Deputy Tom Rachette pleaded to the cloudless sky. His hands gripped his head and his mouth was wide in horror. "This isn't happening."

"Something's going on." Nate Watson, Wolf's long-time teammate on the football field growing up and lifelong friend ever since, stood shaking his head. "Eight votes to none? For that guy? This is BS."

"This is unacceptable." Wolf's mother was shaking, tears in her eyes. "What are you going to do?"

Wolf stood still, eyeing his mother.

"Your father would be horrified. I don't understand. After all our family has given to this county over the years ... after all we've just been through—"

"Don't worry, Mom," Wolf said, because that's all he could think to say. Because since Derek Connell had been announced as the new appointed sheriff of Sluice County, Wolf had been speechless.

A steady stream of citizens of Rocky Points and other far-flung regions of Sluice County were pouring out of the town hall building now, and many of them looked at Wolf with shakes of their heads and shrugs of their shoulders.

Wolf put on his poker face and waited. Gary Connell, the county council chairman and Derek Connell's father, had signaled Wolf to wait and talk to him, and Wolf intended to do just that. The meeting had left a foul taste in Wolf's mouth.

A few seconds later, Derek Connell came out of the building. His thumbs were hooked on his belt, his pectorals were out, and he moved with a heel–toe sheriff's strut.

Wolf hadn't seen Derek Connell's ugly face since a week ago today—not since their *altercation* on top of the cliff, when Derek had tried to push him and Wolf had gotten lucky and seen it coming.

Wolf still hadn't told a single soul about what had happened that day, but now it was apparent that Connell had been filling the ears of the council with a story of his own. One that Wolf hadn't been around to defend himself against. By the looks of Connell, he probably didn't have to work very hard to garner any sympathy.

Connell's face was a mess. Both eye sockets were deeply bruised; a mix of blue, purple, yellow, and green puffy flesh. His nose was larger than normal, split on the bridge with a red horizontal slice, and a large bump in the middle that hadn't been there a week ago. His lips looked like they were in the middle of a particularly nasty herpes outbreak, and a line of stitches above his right eyebrow gave the illusion of one brow longer than the other.

Wolf marveled at the damage, vaguely remembering the repeated elbows he'd given Connell once he'd finally gotten him on the ground. He honestly couldn't begin to guess how many times he'd hit Connell in the face. Apparently it was more than just a few.

Connell's beady blue eyes found Wolf and narrowed. He wiped his nose gingerly and walked over.

"Mrs. Wolf, so nice to see you. Glad you could make it today." Connell opened his muscular arms for a hug.

She turned around and got into Wolf's SUV without saying a word.

"Huh. Okay." He held out a hand to Wolf. "Sorry, man. Better luck next time."

Wolf didn't move.

"Aren't you going to congratulate me?" Connell shrugged and thrust his hand towards Rachette.

Rachette hesitated and then shook it. "Congratulations, Derek." He winced as his skin went white under Connell's grip.

Connell shook for a few seconds too many, his blue eyes boring into Rachette's. He finally let go and walked towards his own SUV.

"Aren't you going to shake my hand there, tough guy?" Nate flexed his chest and squared off to Connell's back.

Connell kept walking and held up his index finger. "Meeting in the sit room at ten. Be there or be sorry."

The SUV rocked as he jumped in and slammed the door. The mystery blond man that had been sitting next to Derek in the town hall meeting was in the passenger seat, staring at them with no particular expression.

The SUV backed up fast, skidding to a halt, then spit rocks at them as it left.

Rachette shook his hand as the SUV turned onto Main

Street with a squeal. "Oh good." He squinted and coughed on the dust. "This is going to be good."

Wolf walked back toward the hall building.

"Wolf!" Nate ran up next to him. "I'm heading up to Laramie for the week."

Nate's tenacity on the football field had never been enough to make up for his lack of size, so he never did play college ball after high school. Instead, he steered his determination toward academia, double majoring in geology and business at the Colorado School of Mines. Now he owned Watson Geological Services, a thriving enterprise that employed forty-one geologists in Wyoming, Colorado, and Utah. Wolf knew he'd be going up to Laramie to help some big oil and gas company for a substantial amount of money.

"All right. Have a good week."

"I will." Nate pulled Wolf to a stop, and then patted him on the shoulder. "I know how much this meant to you. I'm sorry. You going to talk to Gary?"

Wolf nodded.

"Give him hell. I'll see you on Saturday."

"Hey. I'll take Brian fishing with me and Jack this week," Wolf said.

Nate nodded. "Thanks. I owe ya."

CHAPTER 2

Margaret Hitchens stood just inside the door speaking to Gary Connell in a hushed voice.

Turning to leave, she almost ran into Wolf and looked up with a start. "Oh, hi, David."

He grasped and shook her outstretched hand.

Margaret's family had always been close to Wolf's growing up, and she had known his father personally. As far as Wolf had been able to figure out, there had been a love affair that hadn't lasted between Margaret and his father. Maybe when they were ten years old. He didn't know. All he knew is it was before his mother was in the picture.

Despite Margaret's obvious past longing for Wolf's dad, she had always been a good friend to the entire family, Wolf's mother included. Wolf thought her a good person with a sharp wit. She was fun to talk to, and everyone in town considered her *the* real-estate expert.

"Hi, Margaret." He nodded and moved to step past her.

To his surprise, she held on to his hand and squeezed. "Good luck with everything, David. The job sounds great." Then she let go and left the room.

He paused, and then twisted on his heel, but he didn't have a chance to ask her what she meant. She was already out the door.

Gary stood speaking softly, cupping an old man's hands with both of his own.

The old man stood with the reverence of a devout Catholic praising a beloved priest after mass. Three people waited in line behind.

Mayor Wakefield was scooping up his leather bag from a chair and putting it over his shoulder. He noticed Wolf and walked towards him with an exhausted expression.

"We didn't see you last night at the station," Wakefield said.

Wolf nodded. "I needed to get home and take care of some things."

"I hear Julie Mulroy is denying everything Chris told you."

Wolf nodded. Yesterday the mayor's son had shed some light on the suspicious death of a teenaged boy named Jerry Wheatman, implicating a girl in town, Julie Mulroy, as the killer.

"I'm not sure justice will come for what happened. But Chris will be okay. He did the right thing in the end."

Mayor Wakefield gave Wolf an unreadable look, then nodded. "I hope you enjoy your new job. You're going to be missed. I hope you know that."

"New job?" Wolf asked.

The mayor paused, stared at Wolf, then laughed and shook his head as he walked out the door.

More than a little confused, Wolf walked to the now vacant wood seats in the room and sat down.

Five minutes later the doors closed, muffling the outside crackle of tires on gravel.

The old boarded floor squeaked as Gary walked up behind Wolf.

He cleared his throat. "How you doing, David?"

Wolf stood up and walked to the window without saying anything.

People were still milling about in the parking lot, talking in pairs or small groups. Arms were flailing, pointing to the hall, anger creasing their foreheads.

Gary joined him and sighed. "They'll get over it." He folded his muscular arms and leaned against the window.

Wolf gave him a sideways glance. Gary stood looking out with a mischievous half smile.

"Eight votes to none?" Wolf asked.

Gary rubbed his face and looked over his shoulder to the closed door. "I convinced everyone on the council to vote for Derek."

The floor seemed to drop an inch under Wolf's feet. He looked at Gary and felt his face warm.

Gary had just admitted to sabotaging a moment that Wolf had been working towards for years. A moment that Gary Connell knew the full weight of.

Wolf forced himself to look back outside. He could hardly contain the anger.

Gary seemed to read Wolf's expression and shut his eyes. Holding up both hands he said, "Just listen. I know you wanted to be sheriff. But I convinced everyone because I've got something much better for you. Please, don't fret about it." Gary glared at Wolf and put a gentle hand on his arm. "Just keep your cool and come over tonight to my place for dinner. Have I ever let you down in the past?"

Wolf looked at Gary but said nothing.

"I'll explain everything tonight. Seven o'clock. Don't be late." Gary patted his shoulder and walked out.

CHAPTER 3

WOLF PUT his arm around his mother and pulled her close as they looked at the gaping hole in the ground.

The headstone read, *Here Lies Johnathon Wolf. A Beloved Son and Brother.* Next to that, *Here lies Daniel Wolf. A Beloved Husband and Father.*

Staring at the hole made Wolf feel something resembling seasickness, knowing that his father lay mere inches beyond in his coffin, and that his brother would be lying there in a few days.

He leaned his head back and sucked in a breath of crisp air, looking to the cloudless blue sky, and then to the golden aspen trees on a distant mountain.

His breath caught as a memory flashed in his mind. He was standing in nearly the same spot, watching his father being lowered into the earth. It had smelled just like today.

His mother sniffed. "I hate this place."

Wolf scanned the view. It was an endless expanse of pines and changing aspens, spanning a thinly inhabited valley over-looked by thirteen-thousand-foot peaks. Crows cawed nearby as they soared on the wind. Grass and wildflowers swayed at their feet, caressing their shins.

He knew what she meant. "Me too."

He dug in the pocket of his Levi's, fished out the ring, and then held it up in the late-morning sun. Silver with a bright orange coral inlay around the entire circumference, the ring was just as magnificent as the day he had found it lying on his father's armoire, two days after he'd been fatally shot in the line of duty. Since then it had been a personal symbol for Wolf, a reminder of the man his father had been, and who he would forever strive to be.

He twisted it in the light to reveal the engraving inside.

Ayóó ániinishni — 7/21/1985.

Wolf had long ago figured out what the words meant. It was Navajo for *I Love You*. The date afterwards was still a mystery to him.

"That thing again?" His mom reached up and took the ring from his hand and looked at it closely. "I don't know where your father got that. I never did see him wear it."

He'd heard her say that before, and he could never remember his father wearing it either. But it didn't really matter to him. It filled a perfect role in Wolf's life: a reminder of his father, and their distant Navajo heritage. And he wasn't about to dilute the significance of what it had become for him by nitpicking over how much he wore it.

With a flourish, he grabbed it in mock anger and put it on his pinky, the only finger it would fit on.

She laughed. "It looks great on you though."

He laughed quietly and nodded.

A soft throat-clear came from behind them.

Harold Smyser stood a respectful distance away with hands folded and head slightly down. Wolf wondered whether he practiced that stance in the mirror.

"What do you think?" Smyser asked in a gentle tone.

Wolf nodded. "It looks good. Thank you, Harold."

"Yes, thank you, Harold," Wolf's mother said. "What else do we have to do?"

"There really isn't much to worry about, Kathy. We've taken care of everything. We'll just see you here on Saturday morning. We will have everything ready to go. If it's poor weather, then we will just move inside." He pointed his hand at the small gray brick chapel up against the mountain. After that, the funeral director bowed his head and walked away quietly.

Wolf turned to his mother. "What are you going to do?"

"I'm going to go back to Denver. I've been here a few days, and I already can't stand it again." She looked disgusted. "Are you going to get your job back from that ... Derek Connell?"

He lifted his head, shut his eyes, and soaked in the sunlight through his eyelids. "I'll get a guy from the station to drive you."

"No, don't worry. I've already arranged a ride. Some friends drove up here and are in town. I just need to go meet them. They'll take me back. And don't worry about driving me back up here for Saturday. I have a friend who is going to bring me."

Wolf turned with a raised eyebrow.

She looked appalled, stealing a guilty looking glance at his father's grave. "A girl. A friend from the center."

He shrugged. "Okay."

She jabbed him in the ribs and they left.

CHAPTER 4

WOLF PULLED into the station parking lot and squeezed his SUV into a tight spot between two department-issue trucks. A quick count told him there were ten department vehicles including his, which was the entire fleet. That meant every deputy was there, including those who had just completed a night shift.

He sighed and walked toward the main entrance. *Connell.*

When he entered the building, Tammy was gone from reception, so he had to use his key to get into the squad room, which sat empty. He walked to the closed door of the briefing room and put his ear to it.

Silence.

He pulled his head back, and then heard a small cough from within. Pushing the door open, he froze at the sight before him.

The large rectangular table at the center of the room was packed, all chairs occupied, and the head of every man in the department turned toward him in unison with tired-looking eyes. A few straightened up from their slumped positions against the wall, and a gently snoring deputy next to the door snorted awake and wiped his chin.

No one spoke.

Connell jumped up from a seat at the front of the room. "Aha! Okay, here we all are now. We can get started. Thank you for making it to the ten o'clock meeting, Sergeant Wolf."

Wolf looked at his watch. It was 11:44. "What are you talking about?"

Connell pointed towards the wall. "At attention, please."

Wolf glared. "Are you telling me you've kept these deputies waiting for me for an hour and forty-five minutes?"

"No, Sergeant Wolf. You've kept these deputies waiting for you for an hour and forty-five minutes. And each second you talk is another second they are waiting for your inconsideration to finish. So let's get started." Connell turned to the white board and wrote *Sgt. Warren Vickers.*

Wolf let the door click shut and took a spot along the wall.

Connell turned around and clapped his hands.

"As you all are well aware, I am the new sheriff in town." He laughed at his own joke, ignoring the looks of scathing contempt around the table. "I've hired a new deputy sergeant who will be working with me closely to get things going the way I want them. Plus, he is a good man who will be a valuable addition to the department. Without further ado, it's my pleasure to introduce Deputy Sergeant Vickers. Welcome." Connell gave him a nod.

The blond mystery man that had been sitting next to Connell in the town hall earlier stood up. He wore a short-sleeve khaki SCSD uniform shirt, jeans, and a duty belt with a department-issue Glock.

Sergeant Deputy Warren Vickers turned to the men, looking at no one in particular. "How we doin'? Glad to be here." He turned and sat down slowly.

Connell spent the next twenty minutes talking about team-work, and protecting not just the people of Rocky Points but the entire citizenry of Sluice County at any cost, and then going over standard procedures that had been in place for the past ten years. Then he opened his arms and stared the room down. "Any questions?"

No one moved a facial muscle.

"All right then. Let's get back to keeping this town safe. Sergeant Wolf, stay here and talk to me, please."

Rachette gave a nod to Wolf on the way out.

"Rachette!" Connell's voice shook the room. "You've got PT. Get on it. Vickers will check your quota at the end of the day." Rachette looked at Connell, dumbfounded, then shot a pleading glance to Wolf as he left the room.

Wolf offered no reaction to Rachette. He patiently stared at Connell and waited for the room to clear.

Vickers sat studying his fingernails, clearly sticking around for whatever this was. The clock on the wall ticked, and Wolf looked to the closed windows. The room was stifling, and the smell of eleven sweating deputies hung in the still air.

Connell nodded his head as the door shut. "See how it is? You cross me, and you are crossing the entire department. Got that?"

Wolf stepped to the front of the room, and Connell squared off to meet him.

Wolf looked to Vickers and held out his hand. "We haven't met."

Vickers's hand was callused and bone dry, suggesting an outdoorsman, which seemed in stark contrast to the five ounces of hair gel and precise grooming of his facial hair.

Wolf's nostrils burned as he stepped into a cloud of Vickers's designer cologne mixed with Connell's Drakkar Noir.

"Nice to meet you, Sergeant Wolf," he said with a southern drawl. "I've heard a lot about you."

Wolf smiled and looked to Connell, whose face went from

contortion to nonchalance in an instant, Wolf undoubtedly catching him in the throes of some psychotic fantasy.

"I'm sure you have," Wolf said. "I'm sure you have." He looked back to Vickers, then to Connell. "Is that all?"

Connell sneered, furrowing his eyebrows for an instant before relaxing them with a sharp breath. Wolf knew that Connell would be having pain with the stitches above his eye if the cut hadn't yet fully healed.

Wolf thought about the cliff ledge again and glared at Connell.

"You'd better watch your back with this guy, Vickers." Wolf turned to leave.

"Hey, Wolf," Connell said. "No, that's not all. Go ahead and join Rachette today on parking-ticket duty. I know you guys like to be together so much. Vickers will check your quota at the end of the day. Don't be short."

Wolf walked out of the room.

CHAPTER 5

WOLF WAS DRIVING ten miles north of town on the main highway, where the pines thinned out and a vast sage-scrub-covered valley floor began. Cirrus clouds glowed orange with the day's final rays of light, and the fragrant air jetting through the open windows was cooling rapidly.

The radio was loud so he could hear it over the rush of air.

... *Next I'll put on a little David Grisman to help you get through the final leg of your Monday. You're listening to K-B-U-D, eighty-eight point one. Your kindest place on the radio.*

Wolf shook his head. Besides the tasteless marijuana puns, the station always played what he considered to be quality, real music. He turned the fast-picking bluegrass even louder and thought about the situation he was driving into.

What did Gary Connell have to tell him? To offer him?

Today Derek Connell had been appointed sheriff, Wolf had okayed the hole his brother was going to be buried in on the weekend, and he'd been assigned parking-ticket duty with Rachette—a task actively discouraged by former Sheriff Burton, unless there was an event of some sort that would warrant keeping a close eye on parking violations. Wolf figured that whatever Gary had, it couldn't be any worse than anything today had tossed his way.

He slowed, lowered the volume on the radio, and turned onto the gravel in front of the elaborate gate of the 2Shoe Ranch, otherwise known as the Connell family compound.

The right and left pillars that held the thick wooden-beamed crossbar were made of red flagstone imported from the Boulder area. On each monolith was mounted one large sterling-silver horseshoe. A dozen multi-pointed antler racks were mounted on the crossbeam connecting them, and in the middle was a sterling-silver rectangle with a deep engraving that read 2Shoe Ranch.

Wolf wondered how much money had gone into the gate alone as he clicked the music off and rolled to a stop next to an intercom box on a pole. The dash clock said 6:57 and, as was always the case when visiting Gary's estate, the large wrought-iron gate opened swiftly without him having to speak or move a muscle.

He drove fast along the dusty road beyond the gate, winding up a rise that stretched a mile and a half long. The washboard dirt road vibrated the car as he climbed a gradual blind hill covered in sage.

As he came up to the top of that hill, a sight was revealed below that few mortals without large amounts of political or industrial clout had seen.

The main lodge, as Gary Connell called it, was a fifty-thou-sand square-foot log home that was two stories tall in most places, covering a long footprint of at least one hundred yards from right to left. The entire length of the house was well windowed, reflecting the bright orange of the western sky behind him. Wolf knew from experience that the windows were high tech, darkening and blocking out one hundred percent of the sun's rays with the push of a button, if wanted. Probably bomb-proof, too.

Directly behind the property lay a brightly lit pine valley floor that climbed up in between two peaks in excess of thirteen thousand feet, which were part of a vast chain of mountains that extended north and south.

A red cattle barn stood on the right, detached from the southern tip of the house. In between the barn and the house were two smaller red structures. One was filled with farming and ranching equipment, and the other Wolf knew to be filled with mechanical toys—from boats to motorcycles to four wheelers to off-road go-karts.

Further beyond to the south stood a complex of horse stables and a large log house, so impressive in themselves that the rookie visitor might mistake them for yet another wealthy person's property who lived nearby. Wolf, however, knew it to be the palatial guesthouse area of the property.

Wolf drove to the circular drive in front of the main lodge and parked underneath the A-frame-roofed porte cochere. He got out and looked up at the elk-horn chandelier hanging from a thick chain.

Gary opened the front door. "You like it?"

Wolf nodded. "Nice addition."

Wolf walked towards Gary and pointed at his tanned face, then shook his hand. "Looks like you got some sun today."

The interior entryway of the house was a towering ceiling with another large elk-horn chandelier.

"Yeah. Out on the horse all day today. How was your day?"

Wolf shrugged. "Another day on the job."

Gary looked at him for a second and then beckoned with a wave, taking off at a fast paced walk along the front windows of the house.

At sixty-one years old, Gary Connell was a fit man. Though not quite as muscular as his hulking son Derek, Gary was still in impressive physical shape from religious workout routines, and spending more time outdoors than inside. Hunting, ranching, riding horses, fishing, and God knew what else, Gary was an avid outdoorsman through and through. He embraced his accelerating male-patterned-baldness and clipped the remaining hair to the scalp.

They passed more antlers on the walls. More than Wolf remembered since his last visit. It seemed that every square inch of the place had a rack of deer antlers here, a gargantuan set of elk antlers there. The interior of the house was painted with animal keratin.

Wolf looked outside at the fading light, knowing just where they were going. Gary didn't like to do business in any other place of the house.

Gary skidded to a stop and turned to Wolf with closed eyes. "I'm an idiot." He shook his head and sighed. "David, I never got a chance to tell you. I was so sorry ... I am so sorry about your brother."

He placed his hand gently on Wolf's shoulder and looked him in the eye. Wolf always mused at how Derek Connell could have such beady eyes, thinly veiling the contempt for the world around him, while his father could have such wide, gentle eyes, filled with an understanding and empathy that could disarm anyone.

Wolf nodded and they resumed their walk in silence. Wolf knew that the man was being sincere, but he also knew that Gary Connell was making sure all emotional debts were paid, their relationship all square, before springing whatever it was he had on his agenda.

With Gary Connell, there was always an agenda.

The trophy room, as Gary called it, was designed to be an

overwhelming display of money and power to the first-time comer. Or so Wolf assumed.

A green pool table stood in the center of the auditorium-sized space, illuminated by yet another antler light fixture above it, hanging from an impossibly long chain. Huge brown suede leather couches were placed in various intimate configurations around it, lit softly by colorful Tiffany stained-glass lamps on dark wood tables.

A fireplace ringed with comfortable leather seats and tables of all shapes and sizes dominated one side of the room, and a dark wood crescent-shaped bar, backed with over a hundred bottles of only the finest liquor, dominated the other.

Mounted heads of big game animals from all seven continents hung from the three wood-paneled walls high above, and the final side of the huge cubed room was a two-story window displaying the dark silhouettes of the western peaks outside. Classical music played softly through speakers somewhere, everywhere. The room smelled of leather, pine, and fine tobacco.

Wolf made no show of taking any of it in, which seemed to disappoint Gary a little.

Wolf had seen the room before. He hadn't, however, seen the man behind the bar before.

"David Wolf, this is Henry Young, my head of security operations for Connell-Brack Mining Corp."

"Hi." Wolf nodded and extended a shake.

Wolf's hand swam in the massive grip of the much taller man, who looked to be almost seven feet tall, and though he wore a long-sleeved sweater, Wolf could tell from the clear lines of the muscles in his neck and slim face that the man was in top physical shape. Wolf fought the part of his brain that wanted to openly gawk at the man's physical form.

Young stared with calm bark-colored eyes, one of which had

a two-inch vertical scar underneath. It looked like it had been a particularly bad knife wound that had received little or no medical attention. His closely cropped brown hair and overall physical presence gave off the air of special forces rather than circus freak.

"Young here was a SEAL."

Gary paused and looked between them, waiting for a reaction that wasn't coming. He cleared his throat and held up a finger to Young. "Can you pour us three glasses from that Macallan 1939?" Gary pointed to a bottle in the front row.

Young turned to fetch the bottle and dug out three glasses from behind the bar.

"Come here." Gary walked to a frosted glass door along the wall and pressed a button.

Wolf followed.

The glass opened like a Star Trek bay door, they walked through, and it closed soundlessly behind them a few seconds later. Inside, the music played at the same ambient volume.

"Take your pick." He waved his hand at rows of neatly stacked cigars, some in their own state-of-the-art humidor cases.

Wolf shrugged. "I wouldn't know where to begin."

Gary picked two, clipped them with expert speed and handed one to Wolf. "Davidoff. This one will go great with the Macallan."

"Thanks."

They left the room, walked back to the waiting scotches, and sat down on the hand-carved barstools.

Young stood behind the bar, eyeing Wolf without expression.

Gary picked up his scotch. "Cheers."

Wolf chimed his glass against the other two and set it back down without taking a sip.

Gary smacked his lips. "What, you're not going to drink

that? It's an eleven-thousand-dollar bottle of scotch. Do you want something else?"

"I want to know what you want."

Gary stood and walked to the other side of the bar. He pulled out a box of wooden matches and lit his cigar, twirling and licking and pulling until he was satisfied with the look of the ember, then set the box down in front of Wolf.

Wolf ignored it.

Gary glared and pointed the smoldering tip of the cigar at him. "I want you to come work for me."

Wolf shook his head. "What?"

"The reason I asked the rest of the council to appoint my son sheriff is because I want you to come work for me."

"No." Wolf said.

"Listen. Hear me out. Like I said, have I ever let you down before? When your father died, who stepped in and bought your ranch and let you and your family stay on it?" He pointed the cigar again. "Payment-free for years, and then interest-free when you insisted on paying me."

Wolf sat back against the stool, took a deep breath, and looked at two polar-bear heads on the wall. "All right," he said. "What do you have?"

"You would be working closely here with Henry. Now that we've opened our sixth mine, we need more security. But I need competent guys to head it up. You'd be surprised at the kind of shit that goes on in our world. We don't just need uniformed guards at every entrance. I'm talking about clandestine stuff. Real spy versus spy, and I need people with brains leading the effort to keep CBM safe against the competition."

Wolf leaned forward thumbing the ring on his pinky finger. The coral inlay reflected a tight beam of light that shone down from the ceiling.

"I know exactly what you are making right now at the

department. Forty-one thousand dollars. Before taxes. With a twelve-year-old child. Living on a piece of land you don't own." Gary sipped his scotch and set down the glass. "How much is the assisted living your mother is staying at in Denver? My God. How are you living? How are you eating?" He took a big puff of the cigar and looked at him with squinted eyes. Gary put on an embarrassed face. Embarrassed for prying so rudely into Wolf's intimate, personal life, and then he held up a hand. "And now you have that godforsaken incident with your brother in Italy. How much is that funeral going to set you back?"

Wolf looked at Young. He could have sworn he saw a thinly concealed smile.

"Come work for me," Gary said. "You want the sheriff job? Why? So what? So you can start at sixty-one-K and then finally have enough to live hand to mouth? I'll start you at two hundred fifty thousand dollars. Within two years you'll be making more.

"You'll work from just outside town at our headquarters, and travel a few times a month, just to our other mines, which are in Colorado and California. And when you do travel, you'll be in the lap of luxury." He took a loud sip of the scotch and kept his ice-blue eyes locked on Wolf's. "You'll be able to buy that ranch back from me. You think I like owning that thing? You'll be able to pay for whatever college your son wants to go to."

Wolf stared at the glass in front of him, lifted it, and took a sip. The peaty liquid slid down his throat with a gentle burn. It was the smoothest scotch he'd ever tasted in his life.

Gary laughed and stood tall with his arms out. "David, this is a big deal, a big opportunity, and I would be honored if you would come work for our company. Give that piece of shit job to Derek, and come work for me."

Wolf picked up and twisted the glass, looking at the

distorted magnification of his father's silver ring through the scotch.

"There are a few problems."

The silence of the room was deafening. The music was in between overtures, or movements, or songs.

"Firstly, I really wanted that sheriff job. And I still do." He glanced at Young. The man's lip was curled into a smile.

"I don't know why this guy got out," Wolf said, "but I left the army because I wanted to come here to spend more time with my son. I wanted to show him what a good man was. It's not about the money. It's about what I've always wanted, ever since my dad was killed in the line of duty. To be a lawman. To be like him, and to make my son proud."

"David, this is a lawman position. You'll be doing something—"

"There's also one more thing. Something more important than anything else. I don't know what your son told you about what I did to his face. But he got what he deserved that day. If I had let him have his way, I'd be getting buried right next to my brother this week."

Gary stood straight and inhaled through his nose.

"Your son can't be sheriff of Sluice County, Gary."

The music started up again.

Gary's eyes were glazed, thinking hard about something. Then they focused on Wolf and went mean. "So let me get this straight. Your story is that my son tried to kill you?"

Wolf side-stepped off the barstool and rested his eyes on a snarling boar's head hanging above Young's now smiling face.

Gary said, "What my son told me about what happened between you two was obviously a little one-sided. I understand that, David. I know you didn't jump him on the mountain that day. Probably didn't club him with a stick while his back was turned, like he said you did. That's why we never considered raising charges against you, and I told my son to drop it. But what you are accusing my son of goes well beyond what exaggerations he may," he raised his eyebrows, "or may *not* have come up with."

Wolf slapped the bar top and turned away. "Sorry, Gary. I appreciate the offer, but I can't take it."

Gary chuffed. "So that's it?"

Wolf waved a hand and walked out of the room.

Gary's soft footsteps followed Wolf as he marched down the hall, through rising and falling classical music seeping out of log support pillars, through mouth-watering aromas of seasoned and seared prime rib and potatoes, and out the front door.

"Wolf!" Gary yelled from the front doorway. "We're going to have to talk about that ranch of mine you're staying on. I think it's high time I start charging market value for rent, or I'm going to have to sell it. If you can't afford it, maybe you can find somewhere else to live. Good luck."

And with that, he slammed the door shut.

Wolf turned back to his truck and got in. As he turned the ignition, the headlights illuminated a man smoking a cigarette on the edge of the circled drive. It was Buck, one of the ranch hands, staring into the headlights with squinted eyes. Or was it Earl? He could never remember which was which.

Wolf spat gravel from his rear tires on the way out.

CHAPTER 6

GARY CONNELL CHOMPED through the tip of his cigar, then mashed it into the ashtray, sending a shower of sparks onto the bar counter.

His father had been right again, and he'd be hearing about it in a few seconds. Or minutes. Or whenever he finished shuffling his ass down the hall. The rattling cough Gary had heard two minutes ago told him he was on his way.

On cue, the old man scraped his walker around the corner and into the trophy room.

A wide, condescending smile lit up his face. "That went well." He laughed, instantly breaking into another coughing fit. "Put that thing out."

Gary held up his hands, looked to the smoldering ashtray, and walked towards his father. "Why don't you stay in bed, old man?"

Wallace Connell's eyes were pure fury. "Why don't you pull your head out of your ass?"

"Right." Gary walked back to the bar. "You can walk yourself."

Gary sat down and pointed at his glass.

Young stared at it, unmoving.

Gary raised his eyebrows. "Please."

After a few seconds of motionless contemplation, Young picked up the bottle and poured a few inches of scotch, all the while gazing into Gary's eyes.

An involuntary shiver ran up Gary's spine as the huge man flawlessly grabbed the bottle, took off the lid, and poured without even looking at what he was doing.

He was surrounded by assholes.

Gary sat motionless, watching out of the corner of his eye as his father arrived and steadied himself on a barstool, twisting and tipping it, sending his cane skidding across the wood floor. With a grunt and what Gary hoped was a fart, and nothing else, his father got control and perched himself on the stool next to him.

Young sprang into action, pulling out a fresh glass, setting it in front of the old man and pouring him two fingers of Macallan.

"Thanks, Henry."

Young leaned back and stared at Gary.

Assholes.

Gary cleared his throat. "All right. I'm on board. Let's do it."

His father blew scotch out of his mouth and all over the bar. "You think? For Chrissakes, boy. You don't have to tell us. He was wearing the damn thing on his hand!" His father shook, like he always did now, like he was sitting on a vibrating bed every second of his life. "We are runnin' on borrowed time, boys. Make no mistake about it. We've got to act. Tonight. They're getting close down there." He pointed out of the darkened window.

Gary took a sip, and suddenly the five-hundred-dollar pool of liquid in his glass tasted bitter. "I know. I just wanted to keep him—"

"I know what you were trying to do. You've been dickin' around with that boy for sixteen years now. Ever since you made this goddam mess. You're well beyond being able to do the *right thing* here." He paused and turned to Gary. "It's decision time."

Decision time.

Gary had heard that phrase countless times from his father's mouth during his lifelong tenure with the family business. Decision time was code. Code for time to stop being a pussy and man up. Man up and step over that line you think you've established as a boundary you won't cross—to step off that moral high ground you *think* you stand on.

Decision time. Them or us.

His father slapped a hand on the bar. "If he's around when they hit that cave, we are done. This?" He waved his jittery hands to the four corners of the room. "This is all gone, son." His voice lowered. "Decision time."

Gary eyed Young, who was concentrating on the glass that looked like a thimble in his mammoth hand.

His father sucked down the scotch in one gulp. "All right. Are we all on the same page now?" He stared at Gary.

Gary's gaze dropped and he nodded.

"Call Stephanie. I'm going back to bed."

Stephanie appeared instantly, pushing his plush-top-seated wheelchair around the corner. She had clearly been listening from the hallway just outside the vast room, but Gary didn't care. Her bionic ears had heard worse things over the years, and she was paid handsomely enough to hear everything she was supposed to, and to forget everything she was supposed to.

Stephanie moved in quick, picked up the frail eighty-eight-year-old man from the barstool and set him down gently, gathered the cane, and then wheeled him away in brisk silence.

Gary watched them leave the room, longing for the day he'd

see his father's body sunk in the ground, and then turned back to Young.

"Buck, Earl, and I will take care of the construction site." He pointed a finger at the huge man. "You be careful. More careful than you think you need to be with him. He's competent, and he knows these woods, this land." Gary took a sip and narrowed his eyes. "Almost as well as I do. So be vigilant."

Young blew a puff of air through his lips.

Gary stared at him for a beat, and then continued. "When you're done, bring that damn ring to me, and nothing else. No suspicion. No traces back to us."

Young nodded once, put his glass down, and left the room.

Gary twisted to watch the behemoth of a man leave, wondering just what he would do to take care of the job. He didn't want to know. Regret slammed like a lead weight in his stomach. He closed his eyes and took a deep, transforming breath.

When he opened his eyes, he was Gary Connell once again, a man with more power in his little finger than any god these backwoods Rocky Points hicks prayed to.

CHAPTER 7

WOLF PULLED into the gravel driveway and parked behind a giant new model diesel Ford truck. *Wilson Construction Corp* was scrawled alongside the door. It was Mark's truck, the ex-addict construction-firm owner who had latched onto his wife in rehab over the past six weeks. Or had she latched onto him?

Wolf rang the doorbell, reminding himself he was here to see his son. There was much worse he had endured around the world for the same reward.

Sarah's mother, Angela, answered the door. "Oh my! David! Come in, come in." She pulled the door open.

Wolf scrunched his face. "Hi, Angela. I really can't. Is Jack around? I just wanted to—"

"What? Nonsense. Come in here and say hi to us." Her voice was gentle. She pulled him inside, closed the door behind him and held both his arms. "David, how are you doing?" She looked up at him with the same sky-blue eyes as her daughter's. Tears filled her lower eyelids. "I'm so sorry about your brother."

Wolf nodded. "Thank you, Angela."

Jack thumped down the hall and launched into Wolf's side. "Hey, buddy. How's it going?"

"Good to see you, Dad."

"Good to see you." He hugged tighter, almost breaking into tears as an unexpected wave of gratitude hit him. Just a couple days ago he was halfway around the world, unsure whether he'd ever see his son again, and the promise of this moment, Wolf knew, was the reason he was still alive.

"Hi, David." Sarah padded down the hall in her socks, wearing faded jeans and a white tee shirt that showed off her figure. She leaned against the wall and brushed her blonde hair behind her ear.

"Hi, Sarah. I'm just here to see Jack real quick. How are you doing?"

She nodded and smiled warmly. "I'm doing well, thanks. You?"

Wolf nodded noncommittally as he studied Sarah's face. Her skin was tanned and smooth-looking, and her eyes were the blue of a midday Colorado sky. The whites of her eyes were like cream. She looked full of life. She looked good.

Loud conversation between men bellowed from the kitchen, and Sarah glanced over her shoulder, smiling sheepishly at what sounded like a good-natured argument between her father and Mark.

Her mother ignored Wolf's protests and grabbed his arm, pulling him past Sarah, down the hall, and into the large kitchen.

Wolf's mouth gushed with saliva at the sight and smell of open pizza boxes on the counter. It had been before noon since he'd eaten last.

"Hi, David. Good to see you." Dennis stood from the kitchen table and shook his hand warmly. "How you holding up?"

Wolf smiled. "I'm doing all right, thanks."

Dennis held his grip with a sincere look. "I'm sorry about your brother."

Wolf nodded and looked to Mark, who was sitting in awkward silence.

He stood and shook Wolf's hand. "Hi, David. Good to see you again."

"Hi, Mark."

"Sit down and eat. I can see you're hungry." Angela dug a plate out of the cupboard and gave it to him.

He looked at the thick slices of meat-covered pizza in the box. "Uh. Yeah, okay, thanks."

Sarah sat down next to Mark, looking slightly mortified.

"This stuff is probably a lot different than you had in Italy, huh?" Angela said.

"Yeah, it is, but I'm sure glad to be eating it again."

They ate in silence for a bit. Then Wolf fielded their questions about Italy, telling vague snippets of the story, keeping Jack's sensitive ears in mind.

Sensing Wolf's desire to change the subject, Dennis and Angela took over being the center of attention, recounting their harrowing adventures with luggage in Rome, the best wine they'd ever tasted in their lives in Tuscany, and a few other mild tales of intrigue from their voyage to Italy so many years ago.

Wolf had heard the stories before, but still laughed in all the right places as if it were the first time.

Wolf ate his pizza with his eyes down, remembering how he and Sarah had had this entire house to themselves for those few weeks, making love in every single room. Back when they were young and their love burned white-hot.

He looked up at Sarah, and found she was looking at him, undoubtedly thinking of the same thing.

Wolf swore he saw a hint of a smile, which she quickly smothered against her glass of soda.

She looked good.

Snapping out of it, whatever *it* was, he turned to Mark. "So, Mark, what are you working on now? Building houses? Or ..."

Mark flicked a glance at Sarah and cleared his throat. "No. I actually have a highway construction company, and then we also do commercial. I used to do houses," he waved his hand towards Dennis, "but not anymore."

Dennis snorted. "Yeah, now he sucks money from the government. Can't blame him. They pay well."

Mark shook his head and smiled.

"Are you working on the highway expansion in Cave Creek Canyon?" Wolf asked.

"Yes, I am actually."

Wolf was familiar with the project. Everyone was. Cave Creek Canyon was north of town, beginning just past the Connell compound entrance. The steep-walled winding canyon created a traffic bottleneck for the Denver weekend warriors coming and going during ski season. The project was widening the road to two lanes in both directions, and generally straightening it, removing the two blind turns where numerous accidents had occurred over the years.

"And how's it going?"

He shrugged. "It's going a little slower than anticipated. But we'll get it done before this upcoming ski season, that's for sure."

Wolf nodded. The table went silent for a few moments, so he pressed on. "Why so slow?"

"It's tricky country. Tricky ground. It's called Cave Creek for a reason. We've run into a lot of caves and pockets, bringing the ground above them tumbling down, making even more work. Or sometimes we'll brace what we do find so that they won't collapse, which takes time. Some of the caves have already collapsed, leaving scree piles high up the side of the mountain, which we have to clear, then build walls against the new slide area it creates." He shrugged and shook his head, then put his elbows on the table. "It's a lot of work."

"And I'll stick with houses, thank you," Dennis said.

Mark laughed. "Yeah, yeah." His face turned serious again. "It's just tough to predict what exactly it's going to take to finish it until you get digging. But I'm pretty confident we're close."

Wolf thought of how he'd explored some of the caves there with Nate over the years. Then he thought about the location of the construction site, just about a quarter-mile past the Connells' 2Shoe Ranch.

Wolf's thoughts spiraled further inward as Dennis and Mark talked about the intricacies of rates on construction loans, appreciation, or something else Wolf had no interest in. He looked to Jack, and thought of the two-hundred-and-fifty-thousand-dollar-a-year job he'd just turned down. *Over twenty thousand dollars a month.*

His stomach churned as he wondered yet again if he'd made a mistake. Then he thought about how a thousand tiny hairs had been ripped from his scalp as Connell's hands had bounced off the top of his head. Then he remembered the sight of his hat flying over the edge of the cliff.

"David?"

Wolf's eyes rose to meet everyone staring at him. "Yes?"

Sarah was staring halfway between him and her plate, and the rest were staring at him with wide expectant glares.

"I'm sorry, what?"

Dennis cleared his throat. "I was just saying I was talking to Margaret Hitchens today, giving her hell for the whole sheriff appointment thing, and she said that you were taking another job."

Wolf set the crust of his pizza on his plate. "Uh, no. I didn't end up taking that job."

"Oh." Dennis looked confused.

The table plummeted into a deep silence, and everyone's eyes studied their plates. Everyone's but Jack's, that is, who was staring at Wolf with wide-eyed concern.

Wolf winked and gave a small nod, which instantly relaxed Jack, who smiled and shoved half a piece of pizza into his mouth.

Wolf shook his head as his son's mouth bulged like a balloon. "Thank you so much for dinner, Angela." He placed his napkin on his plate and stood up. "And Dennis, and Sarah, and Mark, and weirdo."

Jack laughed through his stuffed mouth and so did the rest of the table.

Dennis and Mark stood up, scooting their chairs back on the wood floor.

"That new sheriff's an idiot and an asshole." Dennis poked the table with his index finger.

"Dennis!" Angela pointed to Jack with a horrified expression. "Where the heck did that come from? And watch your mouth."

They all laughed again as Dennis gave Angela a defiant sideways glance.

"I'm serious."

Wolf stopped. "Any particular reason you are telling me this, Dennis?"

He squinted. "Well, no. I just ... I can't believe he's sheriff now, and you're not. Goddamn, it's about time we start electing a sheriff, like the rest of the free world. It's ludicrous. It's a goddamn—"

"Dad, calm down." Sarah put her hand out towards her father. "I'm sure Dave has a plan to get his job back. Just ... please, stop swearing."

Dennis shook his head and concentrated on his plate.

"Thanks, guys." Wolf smiled. "I'm glad to have you on my side."

After they cleared the table, Wolf approached Sarah and touched her on the shoulder. "Sarah, could I talk to you a minute?"

"Sure."

Mark stood with an awkward expression, perhaps reeling from the family-esque moment that had just passed, and then he smiled. "Bye, Dave."

Wolf nodded and gave Jack a hug. "You want to go fishing tomorrow afternoon? After school?"

"Yeah. Can Brian come?"

"Yep. That's what I was thinking. His dad's in Laramie for the week, so I figured he'd want to come. Probably around three or four."

"Okay."

"Later," Wolf said. "I love you."

"Bye. Love you too."

Wolf ruffled his son's hair and walked with Sarah down the hall to the front door.

She lowered her voice. "What's up?"

"You know John's funeral is on Saturday at ten in the morning, right?"

She nodded.

"Can you put together a list of friends you think we need to contact? I'm doing the same, but I just don't want to forget anyone."

"Yeah, sure. Of course."

He nodded, looking down at her. "Thanks."

She tilted her head sideways and some hair swung in front of her eyes. As she tucked it behind her ear, she crossed her legs and put her hands in the rear pockets.

Wolf couldn't help but glance at her chest. The scent of her flowery perfume, that same brand she always wore, sent a rush of hormones through his body. He turned away and looked out into the night through the door window. "You look really good, Sarah. Really healthy. Happy." He reached for the door.

She stood unmoving, watching him, then lowered her eyes as footsteps approached.

Mark walked down the hallway and put an arm around her.

"I'll talk to you later, okay?" He looked at Sarah. "I'll be picking up Jack tomorrow afternoon. He can spend the night at the ranch if he wants. I'll take him to school the next morning."

She nodded, staring at his feet.

Wolf held out his hand. "Good to see you, Mark."

Mark lifted his arm off Sarah and gave his hand a quick pump. "Good to see you, David."

Wolf left, closing the door behind himself.

CHAPTER 8

Deputy Rachette's Volkswagen Golf sputtered into the station lot. Whether the engine shut down as a result of his twisting the key or just stalled out with good timing was up for debate.

He got out, set his bag of lunch trash on the roof, and glared at the back window. He opened the rear door and shimmied the glass up with both hands, then shut the door while mashing his hand against the window. By a rare miracle, the window stayed up.

Satisfied, he lifted the front door handle and closed it gently. The rear window dropped back down an inch.

"Ah!" He shook his fists at the sky, grabbed the trash and walked away, kicking the rear tire with his work boot.

The pessimism was getting too much to handle. Just a week ago he'd looked at that twenty-one-year-old piece of junk as a rite of passage, a vehicle that he'd surely get rid of when his career moved further along the great path it was on. One day he was going to look back on the memory of the car and laugh, telling stories at Thanksgiving dinners back home of the windows falling down, and the fuel line that froze if you chewed a piece of peppermint gum and breathed on it, and the change bin lid that wouldn't close, and the countless other quirks he had to live with while driving this thing.

But right about now, he wondered if that day would ever come.

He sucked at the iceless Coke until it gurgled empty and then looked at it with a shake of his head. His future was this empty Coke cup, his career prospects the wadded-up bag of burger-and-fries debris. And the piece of crap car ... well, that was his car.

His phone vibrated in his pocket. It was Wolf.

"Hey."

"Hey, what's going on over there?" The voice sounded distant in the earpiece.

Rachette meandered back to the piece of crap. "Just getting back from PT duty. Day number-two of a full week of PT fun."

Wolf was silent for a few seconds. "That sucks."

"Ha. Yeah, you could say that. I can't handle working for this asshole." He stopped and looked to the sky, scratching his head, and then shot a look to the garage door of the station, which was thankfully empty. He lowered his voice. "Correction. These assholes, plural. I'm starting to think about going back to Nebraska at this point. I don't want to go back to that Podunk town, but it's sure as hell better than this."

Wolf's breath was a loud crackle, or it was a gust of wind. Rachette couldn't tell. He set down the trash again and looked towards the pine trees. "What are you up to today? Never did see you this morning."

"Yeah, I'm keeping away from the station for a while."

Rachette tucked the phone under his chin and put a chew in his lip. "I don't know, Wolf. What do you think? I used to feel like part of this team here, you know? And I knew someday I'd be promoted. And I knew someday I would be able to get rid of this piece-of-shit car." He kicked his rear tire, which sent the window sliding down another inch. "But now, it's like there's no future here, you know? At least not for me, that's for sure. Connell made that clear this morning when he assigned me to PT all week."

Wolf said nothing.

"You there?"

"Yeah," Wolf said. "Look, I'm not sure what to say at this moment. I guess I recommend sucking it up." Wolf's voice was loud in the earpiece.

Rachette felt the blood rush to his face as he waited for something more, which apparently wasn't coming. "Okay. Yeah. I'll suck it up. I just ... yeah, okay." He raised his watch and didn't really look at it. "All right, I've gotta get back in the station."

"Listen. Are you going back out onto PT this afternoon?"

"No. I finished my quota this morning."

"Just keep me posted if you guys need any help."

"Okay."

"We'll talk later," Wolf said, and hung up.

Rachette stared at the phone and noticed his hand was shaking. Wolf's words had been like a palm to the nose. Putting the phone back in his pocket he shuffled across the lot to the open garage, shoved his food bag in the trash, and walked inside.

The man was right, of course. Wolf always seemed to take the right angle on a situation. Rachette was complaining, and that never got anyone anything worthwhile. *Time to suck it up.*

As he turned the corner a hand thumped against his chest, pushing the breath from his lungs. Before he could react, his shirt was wrenched from his waistband and he was launched headfirst into the concrete wall. His head connected with a dull thud and a sharp pain exploded in his tongue as he bit through the tip.

He was twisted around and only then did he realize it was Connell.

The new sheriff's thick hand clamped on Rachette's throat and pinned him to the wall.

Rachette tried to suck a breath in, but his windpipe was shut tight.

Connell's face bent close. "You talking to your mommy there, Rachette?" He shot a glance to the doorway.

Rachette's eyes darted around the fleet garage. Only a couple silent SUVs. They were alone.

"I'm going to tell you this once." Connell's breath was hot on Rachette's nose. "Wolf's future in this department is non-existent. You either step in line and stop talking to him," he lifted up on Rachette's neck, "and talking smack about me, and your superiors, or you are going to be out of a job, going back to Shitville, Nebraska, or wherever the hell it is you come from." Connell's grip was relentless.

Stars flashed at the edges of Rachette's vision. He wasn't sure if he was dying or simply passing out, but in that instant he started to panic. Connell was a good four or five inches taller than he was, and a hell of a lot bigger in every other way, but Rachette knew he could lay a good walloping on him if it came down to it. Rachette had been in his fair share of scuffles growing up, and he rarely came out of them without doing some serious damage to the other guy. Then again, Connell was a whole new level of beast.

Connell narrowed his eyes and let go, then jumped back a few feet, apparently sensing that Rachette might attack.

Rachette collapsed onto the cool concrete and sucked in a breath with a long whistle that came from his throat. He clawed at his neck, willing his esophagus to open back up.

Connell bent down. "You got that, punk?"

Rachette stared at Connell's dusty work boots through the swirling stars.

"I said, you got that? You'd better start showing me some respect, right now!"

Rachette nodded his head.

"I can't hear you."

"Yes, sir," he croaked.

Connell turned and walked away. "Good. Don't you forget who's in charge here. Don't you forget it for one second." He walked inside, and the door slammed behind him.

Rachette sat on the floor against the wall, sucking in breaths with greedy desperation, knowing in that instant that he would do anything to help Wolf get the sheriff job back from this asshole. Even if it meant he had to murder the son of a bitch himself.

CHAPTER 9

HENRY YOUNG's training in Coronado all those years ago had beaten the weak, tall basketball-player-turned-tough-guy that he was into less than nothing. Down into a sniveling pile of too-long bones, with a halfwit brain and no confidence. And then it had built him back up, molecule by molecule, into a clever, resourceful machine.

Becoming a navy SEAL had instilled in him a sense of pride and purpose. He'd become a member of one of the most dangerous and feared elite forces on the planet. So when, for the first time in his life, he felt arrogance begin to creep into his consciousness, he was less than surprised. It was the hardest team on Earth to become a member of and he'd done it. He was confident he could kick anyone's ass on the planet and it was a good feeling.

But nothing had prepared him for the killing.

No one had told him about that. No one could. It wasn't something you could describe to someone else until it happened, though many fellow SEALs tried.

He still remembered the first—a nameless gook holding a machete at the wrong angle, at the wrong time. The feeling he had after putting two bullets through that man's heart was much better than any drug or vicious sexual escapade could ever match. That rush of excitement stood as the best moment of his life for a short time, until he killed his first man with his blade.

The feeling of the second kill eclipsed the first by ten-fold. He remembered the Asian man's blood gurgling in his throat as he sliced his blade. The splash of warm blood on his own hand. The convulsions of the man's light body in his other arm as he died.

It had been nothing less than life-changing.

Mission after mission, he'd hoped for that feeling once again, and when he killed, he'd gotten it. Unlike the junkie reaching for that elusive first-high feeling, never to reach it again, every time Young killed, it felt better. And better.

It didn't take long to realize that killing needed to be a very integral part of his life. Like water, or food, or three-hour daily workouts.

Of course, missions never guaranteed he would get a chance to kill, so he began making chances. Time off, no matter where he was in the world, became time well spent.

Of course, SEALS were smart. Smart as they come. So when they began to suspect, they had to let him go. It was fine with him. He didn't fight for his job, or try to explain himself. In the end, he just slipped quietly away with an honorable discharge.

Since then, he'd gotten smarter—or, rather, more refined—at finding new victims, and he never stayed in one place for too long. Young's job at Connell-Brack Mining was his fourth job as a security specialist in the past seven years. Each job, on paper, was better than the last, making it look like he was just stepping up the career ladder. In reality, when he was working at a firm, he was killing. And when the pile of bodies got too big to manage, to grow any more without bringing suspicion, he moved on.

What Gary Connell didn't know was that Young already had another job lined up with a competing mining company, and it was about time to climb another rung. There were too many bodies piling in Gary's derelict mine shafts. His instincts were telling him to move on.

But luckily for Gary, things were finally becoming interesting on the job itself. So he'd decided to stick around for a while.

Of course, Young was taking measures to cover himself. The Connells were one fucked-up bunch.

So the first measure was to make sure this kill was anonymous. He had to make it look like an accident.

Which was boring.

Feeling the final breath choked out of a young prostitute underneath his hand, her pulse on his skin pounding, then fading to nothing? A slow stab of his six-inch blade into the abdomen of a naked body tied to a bed, and the invigorating smell that accompanied it? That was real excitement.

Not that there wasn't potential for this situation. There were some interesting people surrounding this Wolf character. Namely his ex-wife. If Young was careful about things, and he always was, he thought he might be able to get some quality time with her; then he could move on, knowing he'd gotten every bit of enjoyment possible out of this rung on the ladder.

Young adjusted his crotch, his arousal quickly fading as he concentrated on the task at hand.

He stood in front of the house, keeping inside the pine trees, which swayed and whistled in the strong wind. He studied the layout for a few minutes, and then walked to the covered carport. It was heavily tracked with fresh tire marks and footprints in the blowing dirt, and obviously the kitchen door near it was the most heavily used entrance to the house.

He picked the lock in three seconds, and then stepped in. He closed the door, muffling the sounds of the violent wind outside, and stood still. The house creaked and there was the gentle hum of the refrigerator, but was otherwise dead quiet.

The kitchen was neat, cleaned to a perfect shine on all surfaces. It smelled of cleaning agents and spices.

Just then, a gust of wind pushed the door open, hitting him in the elbow and letting in a cool blast of air. He turned and closed it harder until the latch clicked.

He held on to the doorknob and looked around the kitchen again, formulating a plan.

He let go of the knob and looked out the window. Swirls of dust kicked up on the dirt driveway. The cross gate where the driveway disappeared over the edge swayed in the wind. He'd just watched Wolf leave, so odds were he was not going to return anytime soon. If he did, he'd easily slip out the back door.

He set his backpack on the floor and took out the stick-on flash weather stripping. Unsheathing his knife, he cut a precise length and applied it to the bottom of the door, flush with the linoleum floor.

He took out the small rectangular piece of tin foil and curled it into a tiny canoe-shaped vessel. He went to the faucet and filled it with just over an ounce of water, then placed it gingerly against the weather stripping of the exterior door he'd just entered through. His movements were fluid, his hands steady, careful to not spill a single drop.

He bent down and looked toward the light coming in from the window, making triply sure that there were no water droplets on the floor.

He removed the vial of metallic powder and spread a thick line of it four inches from the teetering canoe of water.

The thought of blowing up squirrel corpses with M80s when he was a kid brought a small smile to his lips. He had graduated.

With a spring in his step, he walked to the oven and opened it. A cautious person had extinguished the pilot light already. He cranked the gas and heard the tiny hiss, and then waited for the smell of propane to fill his nostrils. Though he couldn't see it, he pictured it cascading like a slow waterfall out of the oven, billowing off the floor before spreading into a thin pool that would grow deeper by the minute.

He exited the kitchen and into the living room of the house, then pulled the door to the kitchen shut. Then he filled the cracks of the door perimeter with spray foam, which billowed outward before hardening to an airtight seal.

Boards underneath the carpet creaked as his two-hundred-and-ninety-five-pound frame glided through the living room. He unlocked the front door and stepped out, locked the bottom lock, and closed it behind him.

Passionless.

CHAPTER 10

THE WIND WHIPPED across the dirt road, rocking Wolf's old Toyota Tacoma. A barrage of dust flew into the truck, and he winced as rocks pelted the windshield. A tiny crack now would be four feet of spider webbed glass by winter. At least he'd had the foresight to stop driving his department-issue SUV. With Connell at the helm of things, Wolf would surely have to pay for any damage to the vehicle driven off-duty out of his own pocket. With money he didn't have.

The wind was usually a daily fact of life at this time of year, and it had been so windy that it made fishing with Jack more of a hassle than fun. They had caught bush branches and tree leaves all afternoon, and just one fish between them.

Wolf was the lucky one. Jack and Brian didn't seem to mind the conditions much, which turned out to be more suitable for throwing rocks into the river.

"You guys got the gear?" Wolf pulled up to the front of the house, shut off the engine and rubbed his eyes.

He had taken a sick day from work and spent almost the entire day outside on a hike, and then he'd picked up the boys and taken them fishing. He had needed the time alone to think, and now he was in desperate need of a nap.

He got out, stretched, and waddled on tight legs towards the barn. One board of the old building was loose and slapping against the side of it in the wind. He needed to replace some of the wood and add a few nails. And while he was at it, it needed a fresh red paint job.

He knew his father would smack him on the back of the head if he were standing next to him now, looking at the abysmal shape of the structure, but he'd been busy for the past few years.

It sure wasn't going to get any TLC from Wolf now; Gary could worry about the state of the barn.

Brian and Jack slammed the tailgate and followed Wolf, pushing each other and laughing.

Wolf squinted as the wind swirled and battered his face with stinging sand. He sheltered his face with an arm and jogged the rest of the way to the barn.

He unlocked the door and stepped in. The air inside was stagnant and hot, so Wolf lifted a window, letting in a cool wisp of air and whipping up a cloud of dust from the warped windowsill.

Wolf looked at the vacant spot on the pegboard above the workbench. "Jack, go get the fish knife, will you? I think it's in the kitchen. Look in the drawer."

Jack set the fish in the porcelain sink, leaned the rods against the wall, and ran out with Brian close on his heels.

Wolf picked up the clamped fillet board; the fish knife clanked to the floor. He sighed, picked it up, and walked outside.

"Hey!" He held it up in his hand and twisted it.

Jack and Brian were pressed against the kitchen door, wrestling. They looked at Wolf, and Jack took his hand off the kitchen doorknob, and then pushed Brian back towards the barn. Brian sprinted, jumping the corner of the truck, with Jack mimicking close behind. Jack slipped and landed shoulder first in the dirt.

Wolf shook his head. "Hey, the kitchen door isn't closed. It's going to blow open. Go—"

Wolf watched as the door swung open on the breeze. Just then he saw a bright flash from inside it, followed instantaneously by a thundering boom as a yellow glow within the kitchen bowed out the walls, shattering the entire end of the house into an exploding sphere of wood and glass.

Wolf lifted his arms in front of his face just as the shockwave hit him, slamming a searing blast of needle-like debris into his shins, forearms and head. Just before he went to the ground, his mind registered the flailing bodies of the two boys.

Wolf came to with his face resting on the dry grass, his ears ringing a single high-pitched tone. Panic hit him like a bucket of ice water, and he jumped up and ran towards the two boys.

"Jack! Brian!"

Jack lay in a huddled ball, covering his head with his arms.

"Jack, you okay?" Wolf knelt down and shook him.

The kitchen, or what was left of it, was roiling in flames and giving off intense heat. He squinted and looked towards the house, hoping the act didn't melt his eyelids shut.

Jack unfurled from his ball and looked up with bloodshot eyes.

"You all right?"

Jack nodded.

Wolf gave silent thanks and went to Brian. "Brian! You all right?"

Wolf did a double take, seeing the propane tank still intact at the rear of where the kitchen used to be. It was engulfed in flames and the side of it was charred black.

Brian's eyes were closed and he didn't move.

Wolf picked him up, slung him over his shoulder and turned to Jack. "Run! Run! Run!"

Jack responded instantly, running at full speed.

Wolf ran as fast as he could, yelling at Jack's heels the whole time. When he estimated they were at least a hundred yards into the woods, he told Jack to stop.

Wolf set Brian down and checked his breathing and pulse. Both were steady and strong, but a gash had opened up on his head, and he was bleeding. Wolf started when he noticed that it wasn't only a gash, but a piece of debris lodged in Brian's skull.

"You all right?" Wolf looked to Jack, who was staring at Brian. "Jack!"

"Yeah. Yeah. I'm fine."

A bright flash, almost imperceptible, pulsed against the surrounding trees, followed a split second later by another explosion.

"What was that?" Jack's eyes were wide.

"The propane tank." Wolf called 9-1-1 and shook Brian gently. "Brian."

Brian stirred, and his eyes fluttered. He brought up his arm and let out a whine, and that was when Wolf noticed that the boy's arm was bent at an awkward angle at the forearm.

Wolf talked to the dispatcher and hung up, then told Jack to help Brian keep his mind off his broken arm and bleeding head. Satisfied that the boys were doing all right, he stood and turned full circle, squinting into the surrounding trees.

CHAPTER 11

HALF of the house smoldered in a wet pile of black cinders, and the other half stood looking unscathed by the time the RPFD was done dousing it with water. Despite the outer appearance, the interior of the standing half was all but destroyed. The walls were charred black, carpets sopping wet, and the furniture a combination of both.

The land behind the house was also charred black and smoking, because the trees behind had caught fire immediately with the fierce wind, spreading the flames up the hill fast and burning over a hundred acres of pine forest.

Thankfully it had been a late-coming monsoon season in the mountains of Colorado, the moisture-laden wood slowing the fire. And now, at sunset, the air had calmed, and the fire crew just about had the flames under control.

A red-and-white helicopter thumped above the ranch to the top of the hill, where it bombed the smoking forest with water.

Wolf watched Rachette weave his way through the fire trucks and emergency vehicles swarming the property. He caught Wolf's eye, nodded, and jogged over.

As way of a greeting, Wolf pointed at Rachette's neck,

which was red, almost bruised, like he'd gotten a row of three or four hickies. "What the hell happened to you?"

"Nothing. You all right?" Rachette asked.

Wolf nodded. "Yeah. Brian was with us. He's pretty beat up, but he'll be all right." Wolf couldn't stop staring at Rachette's neck. "Seriously. What happened?"

Rachette looked up at the hillside. "Nothing."

Wolf stared at him for a few seconds, then turned his attention to the damage. "This was Connell. This was the Connells."

Rachette looked at Wolf with a raised eyebrow. "What?"

They both glanced towards Connell, who was in the process of yelling at a deputy standing by the emergency crew trucks.

Connell had shown up with the first responders and kept his distance, not speaking a word to Wolf as of yet.

A fireman clad in yellow gear walked towards Wolf and Rachette, shaking his head.

"Hey, Dan. What's it look like?"

"Hey, Dave." Dan stopped and exhaled. "Preliminary investigation isn't telling me much. Hell, you know it was the oven leaking the propane, and that's about the only definitive thing I've got so far. I'll need some more time, and I've got another investigator coming in from Frisco tomorrow morning who's going to help."

Wolf looked to Connell, now standing with a hodgepodge group of uniformed men. "I think it was arson, Dan. I saw a white flash just inside the door, right when it exploded. I was looking right at it. Flash powder, I think. Did you find anything there?"

He shrugged. "There was a lot of heat released in the two blasts, and the way the wind fed the flames afterward, there's really not much left that's recognizable. Like I said, I'll need a little more time. But we'll take a look at that."

"Okay. Thanks. Keep me posted." Wolf stared at the

ground, and then saw the two boys flipping through the air again.

Wolf looked up and scanned for Connell again.

Connell was on his cell phone, and staring right at him. Right at Wolf. It was only for the briefest instant.

Now Connell walked away with the phone against his ear. Then he peered over his shoulder and looked at Wolf again.

"What the fuck," Wolf breathed. "That son of a bitch knows something." He marched towards Connell, and then, before he knew it, he was in a full run.

Connell turned with eyes wide at the sound of Wolf's approach, and then mumbled something into the phone, hung up, and shoved it in his pants pocket.

Wolf skidded to a stop inches from him. "Give me that phone."

"No." Connell stood his ground, his hulking chest expanded. "What the hell you doing, Sergeant? Stand down. Now!"

Wolf dug his hand into the front pocket of Connell's pants.

Connell pushed against Wolf's neck with his right hand. "What are you doing?"

Wolf brought his left arm up, knocking Connell's arm away, gripped the back of his head, then dug the fingertips of his right hand into the notch at the base of his throat and pulled down.

With a high squeal, Connell fell straight to the ground, and Wolf landed hard on top of him. Wolf reached into Connell's pocket again, extracted his phone, and popped up in one fluid movement.

Wolf checked the phone. The last call showed *Dad*.

"Put that phone down now!" Connell shouted from behind him.

The surrounding men stepped away, raising their arms, and

at that point Wolf knew Connell had his gun drawn. Probably pointed straight at his back.

Wolf continued walking away, dialed the number, and put the phone to his ear.

"Yeah," the voice said.

Wolf watched the frantic eyes of a nearby deputy, and then heard the thump of a foot and rustle of fabric behind him. He ducked just in time.

Connell's fist grazed his ear with a whoosh.

Wolf dropped the phone and lunged low at Connell's legs, bringing him hard onto his back with a two-leg takedown.

Connell landed with a grunt and bounced up as if he'd landed on a mattress, then grabbed Wolf's head in a left-arm vise headlock and wrenched with superhuman strength.

Wolf's ears folded down and mashed against his head, cutting off all sound.

Then Wolf's body was airborne as he was pulled up and away by a cluster of men grabbing the lower half of his body. For an agonizing few seconds he felt as if his skull was going to crack like a watermelon, or be clean removed from his shoulders.

Connell's grip finally let up, and Wolf's head slipped free, his ears filling with a cacophony of loud yells, grunts, and the scraping of boots.

They both stood up like wild beasts, struggling against the men, who were now running and diving into the mayhem from every direction.

Wolf sucked in deep breaths and fought the web of arms laced around him.

He wanted to kill Connell. There was no other thought in his mind. Connell needed to be put down. He thought of the boys tumbling through the air again, and the memory sent another shot of adrenaline into his blood. He wrenched himself free for a second, gaining a foot of distance before the men pulled him back.

"Whooaaa, whoa!" the collective mass yelled.

Wolf snapped out of it and stopped himself. He took a deep breath, closed his eyes, and then stood still and calm.

Connell pumped his tree-trunk arms against those who gripped him. Among them was the now red-faced Rachette, holding onto the arm that had been death-clamping Wolf's head a few seconds earlier.

"Get. Off. Me!" Connell bounced everyone off, glared at Rachette and then at Wolf.

No one spoke. The men stood in a loose circle, wheezing and coughing. All were wide-eyed with anticipation.

Vickers stepped in between them, looked to the ground, and held both hands out. "Walk away, gentlemen."

"You're fucking ..." Connell pointed with a clinched jaw. A line of fresh blood dripped down the side of his face from the stitches above his eye.

"Gentlemen." Vickers's voice was calm and assertive. "Walk away. Let it go."

Wolf stared unblinking until Connell turned and walked away.

"Where's my phone?" Connell demanded, pushing Deputy Yates aside and looking at the ground.

A firefighter picked up the phone and held it up in the air, seemed to think better of the idea and passed it to Vickers, who walked it to Connell.

Rachette put his hand on Wolf's shoulder. "You all right?"

Wolf nodded. "Yeah." He pointed to his own head, then to Connell's back. "Thanks."

Rachette nodded.

Connell turned on his heels and walked backwards, this

time glaring at Rachette. Connell raised his eyebrows and nodded his head, then he turned back and continued walking.

Wolf noticed Rachette's hand unconsciously come up to his neck.

They stood quietly for a minute while Wolf steadied his breathing.

Rachette dug in his pocket and held out his can of Copenhagen.

"Quit being such an enabler." Wolf snatched it from his hand and took a pinch.

Rachette smiled and gave a sideways glance to the men milling about nearby. He kept his voice low. "What the hell was that? What's going on?"

Wolf nodded to the surrounding men and two women medics who looked just as pumped full of adrenaline as he was. They all paused their conversations, as if waiting for a speech or something.

He knew that the deputies of the SCSD must have been hungry for leadership they were lacking at the moment. The other uniformed men and women gathered in Wolf's front yard were shaken up. This was not normal operating procedure, not by a long shot.

It had been a foregone conclusion in the minds of ninety percent of the deputies, and all other county employees that Deputy Sergeant Wolf would be the next sheriff of Sluice County. For the past two years, Wolf had been in charge of the SCSD in every sense except his official rank. Burton had checked out years ago, effectively handing the reins to Wolf. But now Connell had snatched them away, and he was already steering the department like an inept child. Things were not just going south; they were already there.

Wolf didn't know what to say. "All right, guys, let's just get back to work."

Wolf watched people scatter with subdued nods and incredulous glances to one another. "Connell was behind this." Wolf rubbed the side of his neck. "Or the Connells. I don't need to wait for the fire investigation to know that this was arson. I don't leave that propane tank on when I leave. Ever. And I saw that flash just inside the door. The tank was turned on, and set to explode. Plain and simple. First they didn't want me to be sheriff of this county, and now they're willing to kill me to get me out of the picture."

"Wait, what?" Rachette frowned.

Wolf told him about the night before—the job offer from Gary, the big navy SEAL, and Gary and Wolf's falling out after he'd told him about Connell's actions on top of the cliff, and then his refusal of the job.

Rachette shook his head. "Okay, listen to me. Its time you tell me what the hell happened on top of that cliff. You bullshitted me before, and then went to Italy, and I just dropped it. I figured it wasn't any of my business. I figured you didn't want to rat out Connell. I get that. But now I wanna know. I *need* to know. I think I'm entitled to a little explanation, and don't just tell me to suck it up again." Rachette's veins were popping out at his temples. "You gotta externalize this shit. Don't keep it bottled up."

Wolf couldn't stop himself from smiling.

Rachette stood with his chin high and chest out.

"All right. Fine. You're right." Wolf took a deep breath and looked up at the charred mountain. "Connell tried to push me off the cliff that day."

Rachette whiplashed his head back. "What? Wait ... what? What do you mean, he tried to push you off the cliff?"

"I mean he tried to push me off the cliff. I ducked. He missed."

"Holy shit." Rachette turned and looked toward Connell's truck as it sped away.

Wolf nodded and began walking.

"What happened? I need details here!"

Wolf shook his head. "I barely remember. I ducked, he missed, so I lured him into the trees, and luckily I got the best of him."

Rachette strode alongside Wolf. "I don't want to be in the same room as that guy again."

Wolf stopped and looked at him. "I don't think you should be."

"Yeah, you don't know the half of it," Rachette mumbled.

"Is that where the mark on your neck came from? Connell? Is that why you're talking like you have a wad of gauze in your mouth?"

Rachette rolled his eyes and walked slow. "He overheard me talking to you on the phone this afternoon, and jumped me in the garage." He flexed his muscles and made two fists. "He shoved me up against the wall and ..." Rachette pointed at his neck and looked into the distance. "I really thought he was going to choke me to death for a second. Then he just let go and walked away."

Wolf stepped back, conviction filling him now more than ever.

"What are we going to do?" Rachette asked.

"There's something going on here, and we've got to figure out what it is. And obviously we've both gotta watch our asses." Wolf walked along the line of emergency vehicles.

"We've got to get Connell out of the sheriff's office," Rachette said. "That's what we have to do. And put him in jail." Rachette's voice went low. "Or kill him."

Wolf turned with a raised eyebrow.

Rachette held up his hands. "I'm just kidding. Well. No I'm

not. You say the word and I'll kill the bastard." His face was deadpan. "I know what's going on here. The Connells are power-hungry bastards and want to keep themselves at the top. Simple as that."

"I don't know. But if this was the Connells, it's clear they want me out of the picture. Maybe that was why Gary offered me that job, and maybe, since I turned it down, now they want me dead."

Rachette looked at Wolf. "Yeah, but they tried to kill you last week. You just said Connell tried to kill you by pushing you off the cliff. Why would Gary offer you a job after they tried to kill you? Why not just skip that little formality and go straight to trying to kill you again?"

"Maybe Connell and Gary aren't acting together."

Rachette nodded and stopped. "Yeah. Connell's always been jealous of you. I mean, let's face it, everyone knows Gary looks to you as the son he never had, and he looks to Derek Connell like the—well, like the dumbass Connell is. Gary's pretty much taken you under his wing ever since your dad died, right?"

Wolf stopped and turned.

Rachette raised his chin high again, looking Wolf in the eye.

"Yeah, he did," Wolf admitted, looking back up at the scorched earth behind the damp remains of the house, then to the orange sky in the opposite direction.

Rachette continued. "So maybe it's just Connell acting alone. He's trying to finish what he started last week."

"I'm not so sure Connell could pull this explosion off. Plus, I'd be willing to bet Connell was at the station all day, or he has some other perfect alibi. I think it was Gary's security guy. The large ex-navy SEAL I met last night."

Rachette kept silent for a moment. "The guy was big, huh?"

Wolf nodded. "Listen, just watch your ass tonight. I mean, really watch it. No going out drinking."

Rachette closed his eyes and turned to the sun. "Oh, I'll watch it. I sleep with my Glock under my pillow at all times."

Wolf gave him a sidelong glance. "That's ... psychotic. But good."

CHAPTER 12

GARY CONNELL SAT on the pebbly soil in between two sage bushes and dug his boot heels into the ground. He propped his elbows on his knees and looked through the Pentax hunting binoculars towards the construction site. The details of the commotion were fuzzy, as it was over a mile away, but he knew exactly what he was looking at. It was the unmistakable shape of another huge excavator sitting on the trailer of an eighteen-wheeler.

Most of the workers were scurrying to their trucks and driving away. They were paying the mechanical beast no attention, maybe leaving it for the night shift to unload, or waiting to unload it the next day. Either way, it was bad news.

"Well, they've got themselves a new horse." He pulled down the binoculars and stood with a grunt.

Earl sat unmoving on his four-wheeler, and Buck was a few feet away, taking a leak against a bush.

Gary put the binoculars away and waited with hands on his hips.

Buck returned in silence, his bushy white mustache

twitching underneath unblinking eyes. He spat a dollop of black chew-spit on the ground and sat down on his ATV.

"Get ready for another late night, boys," Gary said. "Looks like they're back in business. We'll head out after dinner."

Gary's cell phone vibrated in his Carhartt pants. He pulled it out and answered.

"Yeah."

"You heard, I take it," the crackling voice said.

"Yeah. Come over for dinner tonight. We'll talk about it."

A laugh was barely audible through the earpiece. "We're not talking about anything—I've got a lot to do. Did you see the latest piece of equipment they have?"

"Yes, I did." Gary narrowed his eyes and looked around. *Where was he?* "Come on over for dinner, and we'll talk about it."

Silence. Gary looked at his phone. The call was still connected.

"Hello? Listen! Come over for dinner tonight, and we'll talk about it. I'm not going to ask you again."

Was that a chuckle?

"Hello?" He looked at the phone. "Damn it."

Buck leaned over and spat again. "What was that?"

Gary was shaking. He wasn't so sure about Plan B. Or C. Or whatever they were calling the godforsaken idea now. Things were getting way out of control, and he knew his head of security was enjoying it. *Did Young screw up on purpose?* Gary's pulse doubled at the thought.

"Nothing. Like I said, we've got another late night. Let's go." Gary fired up the four-wheeler's thumping engine, cranked the bars and thumbed the throttle to the limit.

CHAPTER 13

THE DAY's light had completely faded, replaced by the rising moonlight, when Wolf pulled into the driveway of Sarah's parents' house.

Mark's truck was conspicuously gone. Wolf had begun to wonder if the man had moved in.

Dennis answered the door and waved him inside. "You all right? What happened over there?"

"Where's Jack?"

Angela came down the hall and gave him a hug. "He's eating dinner. Get in here and have some too."

Jack and Sarah looked up from the kitchen table. Jack's forehead had a long scrape on top of a slight bruise. Otherwise, he looked freshly showered and overall in perfect health.

"How are you?"

Jack closed his eyes and nodded. "I'm fine."

"How's Brian doing?"

"He's okay, I guess. He's got a cast on his arm, and he had to get five stitches in his head. They said he had a piece of wood stuck in his skull."

Wolf raised his eyebrows and looked to Sarah.

Her eyes watered as she turned to rub Jack's brown hair, and then she pulled him close and kissed him.

Angela set a plate of chicken and rice down and motioned for them to sit.

"Thanks." Wolf dug in, inhaling his plate and sucking down the tall glass of water with ease. Angela was quick to bring him a second helping, which he gratefully ate as well.

When Wolf was done, he looked up and noticed the scared look on everyone's face.

"Do you think this was arson?" Dennis asked.

"I'm going to find out tomorrow. We have a couple of investigators going through the scene."

Sarah was staring at him. Her sapphire eyes sparkled as tears welled up. One rolled down her cheek, and she made no effort to wipe it away.

Wolf's breath caught. He didn't know whether it was from seeing her in such a state of concern, or because of her heart-crushing beauty.

"If you don't mind," he said, "I'd like to stay the night here if I could." He looked at Dennis and Angela.

"Of course. Of course, son." Dennis placed his hand on his shoulder. "You stay here as long as you need. And in case you're wondering, yes, I have plenty of ammunition."

"I'm going to call Nate and see if you can stay in his place in Durango."

Dennis narrowed his eyes. "Do you think we need to?"

Wolf took a sip of his drink, scanning the scared faces around the table, and stopped at Jack's worshipping stare. He thought back on the flash inside the door. "Yes." He looked them all in the eye. "But we'll be fine here tonight."

Wolf would just have to make sure of that.

. . .

Wolf put his phone in his pocket and came inside from the front deck, rubbing the cold out of his hands.

Dennis and Sarah sat on the long couch with their socked feet on the coffee table, staring at a muted nature show on the television.

It had been dark for a few hours, and Angela and Jack were already in bed upstairs. Dennis bent forward, picked up a cold Newcastle from the table, and pointed it at him.

"Thanks." Wolf took a seat next to Sarah and gave cheers to her dad. His body ached, and his mind was fuzzy; both were in need of a good rest. He took a long pull of the beer, and decided the warm massage of the alcohol would do for now.

"What did Nate say? How's Brian doing?" Sarah asked, pulling her hair behind her ear.

"He's doing okay. Broken arm, mild concussion, a few stitches, but he's all right." Wolf took another sip and glanced at Sarah, and did a double take when he noticed she was looking straight into his eyes.

She turned away and readjusted her leg so it rested lightly against Wolf's.

At that moment, he was completely aware of her breath, the fragrant scent of her shampoo. Looking at her leg as it pressed lightly against his, he couldn't help but feel aroused at the sight of her taut thigh muscles underneath her white sweatpants.

"Hey." Dennis was leaning forward, glaring at Wolf.

Wolf froze and looked at Dennis. "Yes?"

"I've been meaning to ask you this for a while now." He shifted forward on the couch. "Do you know a guy named Bill Chester? Or William Chester?"

"No. I don't think I do. Never heard of him. Why?"

Dennis shook his head with a gasp and took a sip of his beer. "He's got that property on—"

"Jeez, Dad, don't you ever think about anything else?" Sarah raised her hands.

He paused, not taking his eyes off Wolf. "Anyway. He has that huge property on the east side of Cave Creek, on the side of the low mountain, kind of at the base of Winslow Peak. A thousand-plus acres."

Wolf nodded. He'd seen the property many times. Anyone who was driving into town from the north had.

Dennis looked disappointed. "You don't know him?"

"No, I've never heard of the guy. Why?"

Dennis leaned back and shrugged. "I want to buy it from him, but I can't find him. He bought it back in the late nineties, and then he just let the land sit there. He has the same house sitting on it, an old piece of junk, completely falling over. It's just strange. I guess I was just wondering if you had an inside story, being in the department and all."

Wolf shrugged. "I have no clue. But, you know, I wasn't here much during the late nineties."

Sarah's leg moved away from his.

"I'm telling you, though, that guy bought the land for 1.2 million dollars. And he just leaves it? Never goes in there? It's just strange." He pointed the remote at the television. "I want that property. There's a really good opportunity there, and he's wasting it."

Wolf was in the camp that letting a thousand acres sit and grow pine trees was a fine use for land.

"Can't you just look up the contact details on public record?" Wolf leaned up, stealing a glance at Sarah, who was now glaring at the television as if it were an old enemy.

"You would think. But he's got a paper trail that just disappears." Dennis yawned, slugged the rest of his beer, and stood up. "All right." He looked at Sarah, who was blank-staring at the TV, and then to Wolf. "Well, if you ever hear anything about that guy, let me know." He nodded at Wolf and kissed his daughter. "Try to get some sleep now."

Wolf nodded, watching him leave up the stairs; they both knew sleep wasn't on the schedule for him tonight.

The room fell into a deep silence. Sarah sat motionless.

"Sarah."

She rolled her eyes a little and looked at him. "What?"

He shifted on the couch to look straight at her. "What's going on? Everything okay?"

"What do you mean?" She kept her eyes on the muted TV.

Wolf reached for the remote and shut it off. "I mean, I really need to start getting answers from you about some things."

Her face soured. "Answers about what?"

"All right, how about this? You're sober now, right?"

"Yes."

"And you feel like you've kicked the pills for good?"

"Yes."

He looked up at the full moon in the window above her. "Then can you tell me what happened all those years ago? Why you started using? Is there a reason? Was it something I did?"

She stared at her hands, picking her nails for a while, and then her lip started quivering. A tear trickled down her cheek.

Wolf narrowed his eyes.

"I-I'm really scared to tell you, David."

This was new. "Scared? About what?" He rested his hand on her shoulder, then thought better of it and pulled it away gently. He didn't want to stop the first real attempt at communication he'd had with her in over ten years.

"I-ah" Her voice cracked. "When you left, after your dad died."

He nodded, encouraging her to go on. "When I went into the army."

She nodded, looking up at nothing and a tear slipped off her chin, landing on her shirt.

"What about it?"

"I did something really bad." She looked at him with glistening eyes.

"Okay." He raised his eyebrows.

His phone erupted into a vibrating conga drum ring.

With a silent scream, he dug in his pocket and hit the button to kill the call. "Sorry." He blinked. "Okay. Go ahead."

She rolled her eyes and leaned forward. "David, we have to talk about this. But—"

His phone rang again. This time he pulled it out and looked at the screen. *Rachette.*

"What's up?" His voice was a little hotter than he meant it to be.

"There's been a stabbing," Rachette said.

Wolf stood up. "Where?" He walked out of the room and down the hallway to the front door. "Who?"

"At Beer Goggles. Baine just called me. I'm heading out now to go down. He's there with Connell and Vickers. It happened over an hour ago."

And Connell had successfully kept them out of the loop for over an hour. "All right. So they have it covered. Why are you going over there? What happened?"

"I think the victim is a guy you know. The guy Sarah is seeing. Isn't his name Mark? Mark Wilson?"

Wolf's pulse jumped. "Yeah. Yeah it is."

CHAPTER 14

BEER GOGGLES BAR squatted in the trees just above a sharp bend in the Chautauqua River. It was a one-story log structure with an outdoor patio that overlooked the rippling water. The locally brewed beer, quality bar food, live music, and ambience of the back patio typically attracted consistent crowds of locals and tourists.

Wolf parked his SUV on the shoulder of the dirt road leading to the lot, behind Rachette's silver Volkswagen. Apparently he'd lost his department vehicle privileges while gaining his PT duty.

Rachette stepped out in full uniform. When he shut the door, his rear window dropped down five inches. "Shit." He grabbed the window and yanked up on it, slamming his fingers on the top. "Dammit!" He turned to Wolf. "Hey. How are you?"

"You've been waiting for me?" Wolf asked.

"Yeah." Rachette shrugged. "I just got here."

Their feet crunched on the dirt road, towards the beeping and scratching of police radios emanating from otherwise silent SCSD vehicles, which were packed into every nook and cranny of the lot. Wolf counted at least fifteen civilian vehicles that wouldn't be going anywhere soon.

Deputies milled about next to a few of them with billowing breath that glowed blue and red from the flashing turret lights.

Wolf scanned the men for Connell and found him on the left side, outside his open vehicle door, talking on his phone while a group of four deputies huddled near. There was a man with a large head of hair in the bright interior of his vehicle, slumped against the back window.

Wolf led Rachette to the right, towards the pub's front entrance.

Before Wolf could reach the door, Rachette walked fast ahead of him, brushing against Wolf with his chin up and chest out as he did so.

Wolf slowed a bit and watched as Rachette ripped open the door and stepped in. The door bounced off the exterior wall with a loud clang and ricocheted back shut in front of Wolf.

Wolf opened the door and walked into the stuffy barroom, thick with the smell of fried food and beer. Rachette shot him a glance that contained no apology, and then turned away to scan the crowd inside. The many patrons inside were huddled in bunches, subdued in their movements, but wide-eyed and whispering with one another in excited clips.

Wolf looked through the mass of people, catching the gaze of Deputy Baine, who had his notebook out, interviewing a girl with a serving bib on.

She turned her head at the sound of the door and her eyes widened. She swiveled her bar stool towards them, squinted her eyes, and broke into a small whimper.

Wolf watched as Rachette narrowed his eyes, as if the bar was filled with smoke, then strode over and paused next to Baine. "I got this. Thanks, Deputy Baine," he said as he placed his muscular arm around the waitress's shoulders and pulled her into a deep embrace.

Her head dove into Rachette's chest as he ducked his mouth close to her ear, whispering something that triggered her to shake and grip his uniform in a death clutch.

Baine stood back with arms raised and looked at Wolf.

"Sir." Baine approached Wolf.

"What's going on?" Wolf asked. "Who's that guy out in Connell's car?"

Baine stepped close and looked at his notebook. "At 8:53 p.m. we received a distress call from"—he turned to the young woman, who was now smiling at Rachette, tears still streaming down her face— "that young lady. She was taking out the trash and found a man lying on the ground out back. She noticed blood, and another man lying a few feet away. The second man was her boss, and looked to be unconscious. He was unconscious, and had a knife in his hand. A knife covered with blood." Baine raised his eyebrows and waved Wolf to a door behind the bar. "Want to see the scene?"

Wolf nodded and followed Baine.

Out the back door of the kitchen was a dirt clearing that stretched behind the building to the left. Straight ahead the clearing dropped off a few feet into the river, and to the right was the windowless exterior wall of the kitchen; the edge of the outdoor patio beyond it.

Crime tape circled the scene.

A darkened spot sat conspicuously in the center of the taped zone, along with three bags of trash. Two of the plastic sacks were on the ground near the waste bins along the wall, and one was nearer the door.

Wolf nodded his head at the two deputies who stood just outside. "Mackey, Tyler."

"Sir."

"Sir."

Footprints smattered the dirt everywhere, inside the tape and out.

Wolf pulled the flashlight from his duty belt and walked the perimeter, looking at the ground. "All right. Give me what you've got."

Baine cleared his throat. "The victim, one Mark Wilson, stabbed once in the stomach. Apparently a very bad wound. More of a slice than a stab. He showed vitals when the paramedics took him, but it didn't look good. He bled out a lot here."

Wolf shined his light on the dark circle in the dirt. "How's he doing now?"

Baine shook his head. "I don't know, sir. I haven't heard anything further."

Wolf swept his flashlight beam across the footprints, identifying where the girl had stopped, dropped the trash bag, and scurried back inside. Boot prints of the EMTs and cops were everywhere. Wolf could see scrapes and impressions from the EMTs picking up Mark, and another flurry of prints where they probably picked up the guy that now sat in Connell's vehicle. Then there were dozens of other unreadable signs. *A mess.*

Rachette came flying out of the back door. "Hey, what's happening?"

Wolf stopped and looked at him with raised eyebrows.

"What?" Rachette looked to Wolf, then at the ground inside the tape.

Wolf walked near the rear of the building and studied the dirt. There was a set of deep tire marks that began at the crime tape and stretched into the darkness out of sight.

Wolf pointed down. "What are these tracks? Whose are these?"

Baine came over and studied his notebook, flipping some pages. "I don't know."

"The EMT footprints go right over them," Wolf said. "It's an SUV or truck, pulled up before the EMTs showed up."

The truck looked to have backed in to the spot and then pulled out forward. Wolf could see the front-wheel marks, how the vehicle had twisted and changed direction as it left.

He pointed the beam of light to the left tire marks, illuminating a deep boot print where a person, clearly a large man, had gotten out of the driver's seat. The prints were deep in the pale dirt, and the stride was long. The footprints led to where the back of the vehicle would have been, and then towards the pool of blood, where they disappeared in the cloud of more recent activity.

A returning set of prints led straight to the door, where the man had climbed in and left.

Wolf looked at the print next to his own size-thirteen work boots. The one in the dirt was larger.

CHAPTER 15

"NICE OF YOU two to show up," Connell said, leaning against the passenger door of his SUV in the parking lot. A group of deputies were huddled around him, and they all turned to look at Wolf and Rachette as they approached.

Wolf nodded past Connell to the truck's interior. "Who do you have in there?"

Connell gazed with half-closed eyelids and waved his hand behind him.

Upon closer inspection, Wolf saw that inside was Jerry Blackman, the owner of the Beer Goggles Bar. He was slumped unconscious with his shaggy long brown hair pressed flat against the window.

"What happened?" Wolf asked.

Connell sneered. "Looks like Blackman here did you a favor. Took the competition for your ex-wife's affection out of the picture for you. You should thank him when he wakes up."

The surrounding deputies dropped their gazes, clearly wanting nothing to do with Connell's attempt at humor.

Wolf asked, "Why is he unconscious?"

Connell shrugged. "He was like that when we found him.

Holding this knife, covered in blood." Connell reached into the Explorer and pulled out an evidence bag with a six-inch, wood-handled, thin-bladed fillet knife covered in blood.

Wolf did a double take at the evidence bag. The fish knife was the same make and model as his own. Then again, he thought, it was a cheap model sold at most sporting-goods stores in the western US. Half the fishermen in town probably had one.

Blackman stirred inside the car, pulling his head away from the window. He was smacking his lips and cracking his eyelids.

Wolf stepped to the rear door. "May I?"

"Have at it," Connell said.

Wolf opened the door, and Blackman jerked his head up and fell back across the seat.

"Whoa!" Connell laughed and walked a few steps away, slapping his leg.

"Hey, Jerry." Wolf pulled him gently upright by his jean jacket. "It's Dave Wolf. Can you hear me?"

"Dave?" Jerry squinted and turned to Wolf.

Wolf pulled some of the hair out of Blackman's eyes and hooked it behind one of his ears. Then he did the same to the other side.

"Can I get some water?" Blackman smacked his lips again. His beard was caked with dirt.

"Someone get a bottle of water here," Wolf said.

"No! Do not get a bottle of water here." Connell stepped in, pointing at the cluster of men.

Wolf ducked into the vehicle. "What happened, Jerry?"

Blackman looked around. His eyes widened. "What the hell? Where am I?" He struggled against the handcuffs behind his back.

"Jerry," Wolf said, "listen to me. You're in the back of one of our vehicles. We found you behind the pub. Do you remember what you were doing behind the pub? What happened?"

"What are you doing, Wolf?" Connell bent down.

"What happened, Jerry?"

Blackman furrowed his brow. "I don't know. I was just taking out the trash from the kitchen and ..." He shook his head. "I don't remember a single thing."

"Get out of there, Wolf," Connell said. "He's waking up, we'll read him his rights and take him into custody, and then we'll question him."

Wolf ignored the order. "Nothing at all? Do you remember—"

"Sergeant Wolf!" A hand slapped on Wolf's back, grabbing a fist full of shirt.

Wolf sensed an attack, and turned around and shoved as hard as he could, sending Sergeant Vickers into a sideways stumble so that he collided with Deputy Baine, who caught him and propped him back up.

Vickers stood up and looked defiantly at Wolf's chest for a second, then met his gaze.

"Don't touch me again, Sergeant Vickers." Wolf thought it had been Connell and already felt bad for the man as he watched Vickers adjust his belt, his face flushing red.

"You're skating on real thin ice, Wolf." Connell's voice was menacing as he stepped forward.

Wolf stared, flicking a glance down to Connell's hand, which was white-knuckled on the handle of his Glock.

Connell let go of the grip and dropped his arm, a move that was clearly observed by many of the deputies.

"Let's relax, guys." Rachette stepped forward and put his hand on Wolf's shoulder.

Wolf walked away with Rachette close on his heels.

Rachette caught up next to him. "What did Blackman say?"

Wolf stopped at his SUV and opened the door. "Not much. But I know he didn't do it."

"How?"

"Blackman was drugged, and then the knife was placed in his hand to make it look like he did it."

"How do you know?"

Wolf looked at his watch. "Look, I've gotta go. There's some strange stuff going down, and I need to keep watch at Sarah's parents'." He climbed in and fired up the engine. "Remember, watch your ass. And meet me in the lot at eight a.m. Stay out of Connell's sights. You and I have a lot to do tomorrow."

Wolf slammed the door, jammed it into drive, and mashed the gas all the way down.

CHAPTER 16

YOUNG PEERED toward the quiet house from his perfect vantage point at the edge of the meadow. The moon was behind the thick pines, engulfing him in shadow, and for good measure he wore jet black, head to toe.

His body was exhausted after a long day of hormonal saturation. The earlier action behind the bar had been satisfying, even though he hadn't gotten a chance to kill the man completely, and the sight of Wolf and his family leaving the house in a panic was downright exhilarating.

And then there was Wolf's ex-wife. She had been a surprise. At the sight of her, it had taken every ounce of his self-control to not run and tackle her right then and there in front of Wolf and the whole family. He vowed to himself that he would have her.

His face twisted into a snarl as he thought about the explosion. It had failed, and now things were complicated. He had to admit, though, that a large part of him was glad it had failed. That meant a lot more action for him.

His crotch swelled as he fondled the panties in his pocket—a souvenir he'd retrieved from inside the house that would have to tide him over for now.

He turned towards the moon and flared his nostrils, then bared his teeth and stuck out his tongue with eyes wide. Making the fearsome face was something he'd learned by watching the Maori warriors in New Zealand. He didn't remember the actual significance of the act, other than to freak out anyone looking at it. For Young, it was something he did to get in touch with that primal part of himself. He was a wild animal now, who no one could tame.

With a hard exhale he turned and jogged back into the forest.

CHAPTER 17

WOLF DROVE north with Rachette along Highway 734 with the rising sun blazing into the cab of the SUV. Wadding up an egg-sandwich wrapper, he threw it onto the passenger side floorboards.

"How was last night over at the in-laws?" Rachette yanked down the visor and turned it against the sun with a squint.

"I didn't see anything. But I told Dennis and Angela I wanted them and Jack out of town today."

"And?"

Wolf sipped his coffee and turned down the radio. "They're packing now, leaving this morning. Going to Nate's place in Durango until we figure this out."

"Good idea." Rachette took a pinch of snuff and gave Wolf a sideways glance. "And Sarah?"

Wolf exhaled loud and held out his hand for the can of snuff. "She's been sitting at the hospital all night, and she's still there. Mark's in critical condition. Apparently it's not looking too good."

They rode in silence for a few minutes.

Wolf thought about the night before, and what Sarah had

been about to tell him before he'd gotten the call from Rachette. Had she cheated on him all those years ago? Last night she had started talking about something that had happened when he went into the army, which was strange. As far as he knew, she hadn't started using drugs until years later, when Jack was born. Or a few years later than that, when he'd gotten out of the army and come home.

He'd always assumed it was his life in the military, leaving her home alone with their only son for six years, with only a few weeks here and there for visit time, that drove her to take painkillers and alcohol.

Or he'd assumed it was when he'd come back. He'd been so ashamed of the way he'd acted when he got home that he'd scarcely allowed himself to think about those few months. The bad dreams, the way he'd woken up screaming, scaring his family witless. That would be enough to drive any wife to popping pills. But she was talking about something that had happened before that part of their life. She was talking about when he went into the army. Before any of the soul-altering stuff had happened to him.

"Wolf?" Rachette was looking at him expectantly.

"Huh?"

"I asked why you think Blackman was drugged. And last night you said he didn't do it."

Wolf shifted in his seat, adjusting the rearview. "Did you see the way he was acting when he came to? Looked like barbiturates. Sedatives. There's only one way to administer fast-acting, long-lasting sedatives—by needle. When I was brushing his hair out of his face last night, I saw a needle mark on his neck, plain as day. Whatever it was will be in the blood-test results."

Rachette scratched his chin and looked into the distance. "Blanche said that Blackman went to take the trash out and never came back. She said she was going to check on him and take out some more trash, and then she found him."

"Yeah. Blackman never got a chance to put that trash in the bins. Remember those two bags sitting on the ground next to them? He must have been drugged right then."

They drove in silence for a few seconds.

Wolf stared at Rachette. "Blanche?"

Rachette raised an eyebrow and looked at Wolf. "Yeah. She's my lady."

Wolf drove for a minute and looked at Rachette. "Your lady?"

Rachette put the visor up, closed his eyes, and turned his face to the sun. "Yeah."

Wolf nodded to himself. "How come you haven't told me about her before?"

Rachette looked at Wolf. "So, where are we going? The Connell compound?"

Wolf sipped his coffee. "There were Sasquatch-sized footprints coming out of the truck that made those tire marks up behind the bar. The only guy that could have made those footprints is that guy, Young, our new navy SEAL friend in town.

"I'd say Young abducted Mark from somewhere else," Wolf continued, "then to that spot at the back of the building. Then he set it up to look like Mark was stabbed there by Blackman."

Rachette thought silently for a few seconds. "But why?"

"With how much Mark bled out in the back of the pub, he must have been stabbed right there. Otherwise, he would have been found dead, and there would have been less blood. Which means he was probably knocked out and kept in the back of Young's truck until it was time to set it up. They're going to find the same stuff in Mark's blood as was in Jerry Blackman's."

"But why set up Jerry Blackman? Why stab Mark in the first place?"

Wolf shrugged. "Young could have been parked on the blind side of that bar for a while, looking for the perfect person to set up. Or just any person to set up. He sees Blackman come out with the trash, hits him with the needle, sets up the whole thing in a few seconds."

Rachette shook his head. "Why would Young try to kill Mark? What does Mark have to do with any of this?"

Wolf shrugged. "I don't think we're going to get any answers from Mark, either. If he isn't dead already, he's going to be nearly there for at least a few days."

Rachette shifted uncomfortably in his seat and shielded the sun with his hand as they approached the gateway to the Connells' 2Shoe Ranch.

"I—Do you think ... Shouldn't we go over our plan here? You know, before we storm the Connell castle?"

Wolf passed the gate at sixty-five miles per hour. "We're going to the Cave Creek construction site."

Rachette whipped his head, and then turned back to Wolf. "Why?"

"Mark's been working the project all summer, and was working there all day yesterday."

Rachette relaxed against his seat. "Good idea."

CHAPTER 18

WOLF PARKED the Explorer outside the chain-link fence next to a Ford F-350 painted with the same construction company logo Mark Wilson had on his truck door.

Wolf pushed down his buffalo felt Stetson, zipped his jacket high, and shoved his hands in his pockets. Frost crunched under their boots as they walked through the wide-open chain-link gate.

The sun was fully up over the peaks and the western slopes of the steep hills were warming in the sun. However, the construction site was still in shadow, and had yet to defrost from the overnight freezing temperatures.

A few men were huddling in a circle, sipping coffee and smoking cigarettes. Why they weren't in the sun by the trucks was a mystery.

"Howdy, officers." One of them tipped his head while the others shuffled their feet.

Wolf extended a hand. "I'm Sergeant Wolf. This is Deputy Rachette."

The head-tipper stepped forward. "I'm Jesse. Glad to see you guys. We thought you weren't going to come after all."

Wolf and Rachette exchanged a glance. "What do you mean?"

Jesse tilted his head to the side. "The vandalism?"

Wolf shook his head. "You're going to have to elaborate."

"We called you guys about some vandalism yesterday. A few times. And you guys never showed up."

Jesse looked between Wolf and Rachette and narrowed his eyes. "You guys have no idea what I'm talking about, do you?"

"No, sorry. We don't. Why don't you show us what you mean," Wolf said.

Jesse broke away from the group and started walking, and Wolf and Rachette followed, leaving the other men behind.

The valley was tight, with steep hills on either side, the rushing Chautauqua river cutting through the middle. The dirt they walked on was graded flat, where the old highway had been completely removed. The expansion and straightening process was well underway, with a straight gouge cut into the rock and dirt slope.

Jesse led them to a yellow excavator. The main operator house sat on top of a continuous track that reminded Wolf of tank tread. He stopped and pointed at the large boom arm. It was peaked at an angle, with its toothed bucket stabbing halfway into the ground near a sheer rock wall.

On the boom, spray painted in runny black paint, was a penis. *Suck my balls* was scrawled on the side of the operator's cab in the same black print.

Wolf nodded. "Aha."

"Yeah. And it's the same on the other side, and the other two machines have the same thing on them." Jesse raised his eyebrows. "And there's some serious damage to them."

"You mean, besides the ... uh ..."

Jesse waved a hand and hopped onto the track with a grunt. Rachette and Wolf followed him up.

There was a gash in the metal tubing that housed the hydraulic piston of the boom.

Wolf bent down to examine it.

"Can you believe that?" Jesse asked, bending down next to him.

The hydraulic piston housing had a gash in it, as if cut open like an aluminum can. But it was thick industrial-strength steel, meant to withstand thousands of pounds per square inch of pressure inside it.

Wolf thumbed the gash. "These kids had some seriously high-powered equipment, I'd say."

"Like I said: some serious damage," Jesse said. "If they would have just cut the hydraulic lines, which they also did, by the way, we would have been up and running yesterday. But this is going to need some serious repair. Welding, new parts, a lot of hard labor. There's no way an axe would go through that. They must have had some hydraulics of their own."

Wolf nodded. "I agree. Nothing less than a hydraulic cutting tool could do that kind of damage." Wolf stood up and looked around. There was another excavator parked nearby with the same paint job. Even from a distance, he could see the similar gash in the hydraulic cylinder.

"The other side piston has the same damage. All the other machines are the same."

They jumped down.

Wolf looked to Jesse. "Please excuse the question, since you've already told us, but, when did this happen?"

"Two nights ago. Monday night. We came into work yesterday morning, and it was like this."

"You have anyone who would want to do this? Any, I don't know, enemies? Jealous rival firms?"

Jesse laughed and shook his head. "I don't think so. But you'd have to ask Mark when he gets here."

Wolf pushed back his hat and cleared his throat. "That's actually what we came to talk to you guys about. Mark's been stabbed."

Wolf watched the genuine reaction of surprise on his face. "What? When?"

"Last night," Wolf said.

Jesse stared at the ground, then back to Wolf. "Is he all right?"

"He's in critical condition. He's at the County General Hospital, about forty miles south of here."

Slowly, Jesse took off his hard hat and shook his head. "That doesn't make any sense. Was he stabbed here?" He craned his neck and looked at the men in the distance.

"Why do you ask? Do you know what Mark was doing last night? After work?" Rachette asked.

"We all left at sundown. We just got the new excavator in, and we'd been doing manual stuff all day waiting for it." He twisted and pointed to the large white excavator—the only one without any vandalism done to it. It was parked near what looked to be a rockslide. "Mark was going to run it for a few hours on his own. He told us all to go home." He held out his hands. "So we did."

Wolf tilted his hat against the sun finally peeking over the hill and looked at the excavator. Walking over to it, he asked, "What are you guys doing here?"

"Well, we're expanding the highway—"

"No, I mean here. With the excavator. What have you guys been specifically working on?"

"We were taking away that scree pile. We started that last week. Then they came and did this on Monday night, and we've been sittin' on our hands ever since." He pointed at the side of the hill. "It looks like Mark didn't get much done here last night."

Wolf noticed two gaping holes in a sheer cliff face forty or so yards down the road.

Jesse saw Wolf looking toward the caves. "Cave Creek. They don't call it that for nothing. This section of the valley has a lot of corridors carved out by water millions of years ago. Some of them have caved in." He pointed back up at the rocks. "A lot of erosion happening here over the years. This was a big rock-slide fifteen or so years ago. We're just pulling away the rock from the bottom until it's gone, then putting up a permanent wall to stop it from happening again."

Wolf nodded.

"Are environmentalists pissed off about this expansion?" Rachette asked.

Jesse shrugged. "They're always pissed off at everything we do. But we've never had any issues with them before. They didn't really make any noise with this particular project either."

They turned to the sound of gravel popping under tires outside the fence.

A department Ford Explorer bounced to a skidding stop next to Wolf's, and Connell got out of the driver's side while Vickers stepped out opposite.

"Howdy, gentlemen." Connell tipped his cowboy hat as he strode through the fence gate. Vickers was close behind, nodding to the men.

Wolf, Rachette, and Jesse walked towards them.

Connell's eyes quickly swept the scene, then locked on Rachette. "Deputy Rachette, what are you doing here? I remember assigning you to PT for the rest of the week." He smiled to himself and then glared at the circle of men. "Who's in charge here?"

Jesse looked from Wolf to Connell. "Hello ... uh, Officer." He stepped forward with an extended arm.

Connell tapped his badge. "Sheriff."

"Sorry, Sheriff. Nice to meet you."

Connell shifted his expression to somber. "I take it you boys have heard about your boss?"

"I was just getting done telling Jesse here about it, Sheriff." Wolf gestured to the other men. "We haven't had a chance to tell everyone else."

Connell glared at Wolf, then looked to the group of men. "Your boss was stabbed in town last night."

Wolf motioned to Rachette, tipped his hat to Jesse and the men, and walked away quietly while they talked.

Rachette shuffled up next to him. His voice was low. "We're just gonna leave them with Connell?"

"Yeah. Why, you wanna stick around?"

"Sergeant Wolf, Deputy Rachette!" Vickers jogged up from behind.

Rachette stopped and turned around and Wolf kept walking.

"Sergeant Wolf."

"What is it, Vickers?" Wolf slowed and turned around.

"Look, I didn't mean to start any beef with you last night, all right?"

Wolf said nothing.

"I'm just trying to follow procedure. I don't want anybody in trouble. I was looking out for everybody."

Wolf walked to his door and opened it. "Is that it?"

Vickers hooked his thumbs on his belt and stepped forward. "I don't know where you were yesterday, and I guess it's fine, with all you got going on lately and all, but we've got a meeting at the station at ten a.m. Lots to cover after last night."

Wolf got in and shut the door, fired up the engine, and rolled down the window. Rachette scurried around the bumper and got in.

"We're not going to be at the station today, Vickers. I can

think of a thousand better things for us to be doing with our time than listening to that guy pretend like he's leading this department. And Rachette's not going to be bringing you any parking tickets later."

Vickers stepped back and glared as Wolf backed up and sped away.

CHAPTER 19

GARY SAT high on the hill in the shade of the pine trees. He twirled the black, shiny piece of tubing in his right hand, made of an inner rubber hose, sheathed with a metallic braiding. In his left was a heavy-duty twist-on cap—two pieces taken from the new excavator before dawn, rendering it useless, or so Buck had insisted.

Buck and Earl stood silent behind him as they all watched the final truck leave to the south in a cloud of dust.

The construction crew hadn't even tried to start the thing up. And why would they? The owner of the company was in the hospital on his deathbed. They had to pay their respects, and they would be wondering if they even had a job.

But they might be back.

And watching Wolf snoop around with that little shit—Rachette was his name—had made him uneasy. Wolf had looked long, right at the spot.

Then Derek had shown up. Seeing him only added to the acid build-up in his gut. In fact, the sight of Derek crippled him with what he could only describe as panic. It was something he'd never felt, and hoped to never feel again. He was glad Buck and Earl were well behind him as they perched on the hillside.

In the end, he'd fought back the foreign bodily reaction with a steeled mind. Just like he'd done in Africa, facing down that charging lion—facing certain doom, shouldering his rifle, aiming, and making the perfect shot. Just like that, he would execute the plan laid forth, tying up all the pesky loose ends of his life in one fell swoop.

Decision time.

"I just hope the state don't bring in another crew and start workin'," Buck said.

Gary laughed and looked down at the construction site, now littered with derelict machines. "You're worried about the government coming in with a crack team of workers to finish the job? That, boys, is not one of our worries."

He stood up and bounced the parts in his hands. "No, I think we've just cleared out this here construction site for at least a week. That crew's not coming back. Their jobs are hanging in the balance down at County General. And if Young completes his task tonight," Gary turned away and swallowed, "there's going to be a hell of a lot of distraction, and we'll have the time to get this godforsaken mess over and done with."

CHAPTER 20

WOLF SQUINTED to see through the windshield into the night outside. Slowing to a stop, he pulled the SUV off the dirt road. A few miles back he'd killed the headlights, and his eyes were now well adjusted, allowing him to squeeze into a jet-black copse of trees without scratching paint.

He switched off the cab light, got out, shut the door softly, and listened. There was no sound, save the faint tick and hiss of his SUV's oil pan and a few crickets.

His feet scraped softly on the smooth dirt road as he walked in the pale light of the waxing almost-full moon. As he passed a dimly lit property on the left, his pulse jumped at a faint rustling. A deer brought its head up and stared at him, snorting and twisting one ear before resuming its evening stroll.

Wolf lowered his Glock, only then realizing he'd pulled it. He slotted it in the less bulky belt-holster—a piece of equipment he'd gotten earlier from home, along with the dark outfit he wore now.

He took a deep breath and continued up the road. It had been a long day on top of a long week and sleep deprivation was beginning to dull his reactions.

Earlier that afternoon, the arson investigator from Frisco had confirmed his suspicions, finding traces of spray-in insulation on the interior door and flash powder at the entrance. Wolf had known what he'd seen, but hearing it officially declared arson felt like validation for insisting so harshly that Sarah's parents take Jack out of town.

Wolf had then made the drive to see Mark at County General, where Sarah stayed glued to his bedside, unable or unwilling to speak much to Wolf.

The doctors seemed hopeful for the man's recovery, as his steady decline had ceased. More than Mark's health, Wolf was concerned for Sarah. Just to make sure she was safe, he'd called in a deputy and made sure that security kept an eye out for any abnormally tall muscular men, and then moved on with his day.

Now he walked along the dark deserted road through the dense forest—in need of some answers, and ready to do whatever it took to get them.

He traveled a further quarter-mile along the quiet road and reached another property. Once there, he stopped, turned a slow circle, and ducked into the woods.

Wolf knelt on one knee at the edge of a manicured lush green backyard lawn surrounded by dense pines and shoulder-height underbrush. Derek Connell's home squatted completely dark in the otherwise bright night. He turned his head slowly, looking and listening for movement. Through a bare gap in the trees, Wolf could see a sliver of twinkling yellow and blue lights of the town below.

He shifted his weight and pine needles crackled under his boot, barely audible over the symphony of crickets. He touched the back of his hand to a tree trunk, coming away with a dollop of sap on his skin. Wiping it on the leg of his cargo pants, he moved closer toward the darkened house.

CHAPTER 21

YOUNG WAITED.

The second he saw, the second he knew what he was seeing, a wash of endorphins flooded his entire body. The movement was subtle, but once he saw it, the unmistakable shape took form.

He opened his mouth in an O and took a slow, deep breath.

It had just been so long, and the past two nights had given him some serious action, and here was more coming.

He looked down at the motionless form on the floor and tongued the split on the inside of his lip. The taste of blood injected another batch of hormones into his veins.

The stabbing last night had given him such a thrill, then seeing her. And now tonight. This was going to be infinitely more fun. He could hardly contain himself. He wanted to scream. His body zinged with anticipation.

He blanked his face, wiping any emotion from his mind, and then he darted into action.

CHAPTER 22

WOLF WAITED motionless next to a tree at the edge of the lawn for twenty minutes. His vision was finally fully adapted to the dark, but no matter how long he stared, he saw no movement within Connell's house. Connell's SUV was parked at the side of the property. Maybe he was out with a friend who had come to pick him up, like Vickers, or a woman. Wolf couldn't picture, and decided he didn't *want* to picture, the type of woman who would date a man like Connell.

Then, finally, a light went on at the far right end of the house, then a fainter light just to the left, and then yet another light.

Wolf felt like he was grasping at straws with the simplicity of his plan, which was to get Connell on record saying something; but then again, Connell was just the type of person who would say something incriminating in a fit of rage. If anything had been proven about Derek Connell over the years, it was that he acted in the heat of the moment, always letting quick emotional reactions win out over better judgment.

Wolf swiveled one hundred eighty degrees to face the dense forest behind Connell's property, and took out his cell phone.

He hunched low to block any visible light emission that might be coming off the screen and scrolled through the menus. After a little navigation, he started the recording function on the smartphone. The timer in the corner began ticking. He locked the phone and shoved it in the breast pocket of his Carhartt jacket, and zipped it shut.

Now he needed some luck.

Wolf turned back and focused on the windows at the rear of the house. A few of them were obscured by now glowing drapes, and one single bay window was unobstructed, giving the only clear view inside. He needed to get closer.

He slid to his left a few yards inside the tree line, keeping an eye on the windows for any movement, then crept through the manicured lawn to the back wall of the house.

He reached the rear of the building and leaned his ear against the cool siding. He heard the soft creak of footfalls inside, what sounded like a cupboard being closed, and then a prolonged silence.

He glided slowly along the back wall, making his way closer to the bay window with each step. As he moved forward, more and more of the interior came into view.

He saw the kitchen first. There was a bright overhead light on and an open cupboard.

Wolf paused, letting a full minute pass. There was still no movement. Nobody in the kitchen.

Wolf palmed the handle of his Glock and stepped further, seeing more of the inside. He viewed the living room on the other side of the glass. Nobody seemed to be there, the chairs and couches empty, though a lamp was dimly lit in the corner.

He sucked in a breath as realization hit him like a rock in the face.

What he'd assumed was a dark-colored area rug in the lower

part of his peripheral vision was Connell, lying face down on the floor.

Adrenaline exploded in his veins as he jerked himself back.

"Gotcha." The deep voice was so close that he felt the scratch of facial hair and warm breath on his earlobe. His gun arm felt like it was ripped out of its socket as his head was wrenched forward in a painful contortion.

Something stung his neck, and then warm invisible pillows crushed inward through his entire body. His vision darkened and swirled, and then all went black.

CHAPTER 23

WOLF LAY in the warm sun. He moved his hands, feeling the smooth, wet sand in between his fingers. Soothing sunlight heated his cheek and the back of his neck.

The mission had gone terribly wrong. There had been so much unanticipated blood, and then there was what he'd had to do. Who he'd had to shoot dead to save the others. The kid couldn't have been more than eight years old. Not much older than his son at home.

But it didn't matter now. The gentle kiss of the breeze on his cheek sent him deeper into thoughtless relaxation. The past was gone. His sins were forgotten again.

Then a cold wave crashed over his head, shocking him onto his elbows. Water streamed off his face and out of his nostrils. He coughed, struggling to take an unobstructed breath of air.

Then another freezing wave hit him. Water plunged into his ear, all the way to the eardrum. He shook his head to clear it and blinked his eyes.

His fingers dug into the warm, wet carpet. *Carpet?* Wolf looked at his left hand. It was glistening.

The fresh coppery scent filled his nostrils. He stared at his arm resting in a red pool, and put concepts together.

It was warm. It was blood.

He shook his head, and then stared at his hand for a while.

Another cold splash hit him in the right side of his face.

"Wake up."

Wolf coughed, blinked hard and turned to see a giant black boot standing next to him, just outside the puddle.

"What the—" A loud slap jarred the back of his head.

"Wake up! You've only got a few minutes." The boots stepped away, opened the door, and left.

Wolf stared at the closed door. His head swam in confusion. Where was he? Who was that? He decided he was too tired to care, so he put his head back on the carpet.

His face squashed into the wet carpet once again, which sent a jolt of electricity through his body. He jumped to his hands and knees and took a sharp breath.

Then he saw Connell, who lay on his back in a huge puddle of blood, with arms and legs splayed out in a starfish position. His eyes were wide, staring up into oblivion.

There were two neat holes in his forehead, and what looked to be at least three in his chest. Blood had splattered against the wall above him.

The heavy feeling of Wolf's body was almost too much to bear. Pins and needles jabbed into every muscle he moved, but coherent thoughts were finally beginning to surface.

There was his gun sitting on the floor. He picked it up, sat back on his heels, and removed the magazine with bloody half-numb fingers. Five shots had been fired.

He stood up, and then stumbled back, realizing that his left boot was standing in the glistening puddle. It left a clear red boot print on the otherwise immaculate cream-colored rug. But actually, he realized, his boot prints were everywhere.

There were also shell casings. He saw three in plain sight, strewn about on the floor. That meant there were at least two more unaccounted for.

His breast pocket began vibrating and making a strange conga drum noise. He ignored it and kept concentrating on piecing things together. This puzzle was important, he thought.

He opened his right hand and twisted it. There were no marks, but it smelled faintly of gunpowder. Somehow he knew he'd fired the gun that had put Connell in a dead heap.

The man who just left.

Wolf set down the gun, unzipped his breast pocket and looked at his phone. There were two missed calls from Rachette displayed on the screen.

He unlocked it, fumbled through the menus with his clean hand and called him.

"Wolf!"

"Hey." His mouth felt full of chalk. He cleared his throat and walked to the kitchen sink, leaving a boot print every other step along the hardwood floor.

"What's going on? You still asleep? I've been calling you for the past few minutes."

Wolf drank long from the faucet.

"Wolf?"

"Yeah, sorry. What's going on?" He felt the nourishing water travel through his body, bringing cold alertness to his brain. "What's up?"

"There's been a report of shots fired at Connell's."

Wake up. You've only got a few minutes.

His heart was racing, his breathing accelerating even harder. His sluggish mind put the pieces all together once again, and once again another shot of adrenaline coursed through his system.

"Wolf?"

"Yeah. Sorry. All right. I'll see you there."

"Okay. First responders are on their way. I'm leaving now. How far out are you? Do you want to pick me up on the way?"

"Uh, no. I'll have to just see you there."

Wolf turned the water to hot and scrubbed his hand clean, then raced back to his gun, holstered it, and left using the back sliding glass door off the kitchen.

He stepped off the deck into thin air and fell hard onto his shoulder, stabbing more pins and needles through his muscles. As he struggled to get up, he heard a faint cop siren, growing louder by the second.

He crashed through the underbrush perimeter of the back yard, through the dark pine trees, and burst out onto the dirt road with a skid, almost twisting his ankle. Without thinking, following some deep instinct, he gritted his teeth and ran.

His bouncing vision focused on the dirt road as he sprinted as fast as he could, and the only sound he could hear now was his rapid breath, wheezing in and out of his mouth. There was a part of his brain that was screaming for him to calm down, but another part was winning out, pushing him to run and not look back.

About a quarter-mile down the road the trees began flickering red and blue, and then a set of headlights burst on the horizon.

Wolf turned and stumbled off the road. He cried out as he crashed into a low hanging branch and flopped onto his back. Ignoring the now burning pain across his chest, he rolled onto his hands and knees and shuffled behind a tree trunk just in time.

A low roar of tires and ear-splitting sirens approached fast, and then dropped in pitch as two speeding SCSD SUVs passed by.

Wolf squinted and put his mouth on his sleeve as the air

whipped into a dusty vortex. He wasted no time sprinting back onto the road, taking advantage of the smokescreen.

He ran down the road as fast as he could, not daring to look back to see whether brake lights were blooming or not. He finally reached his car and collapsed onto his knees next to the driver's side door. His stomach twisted and convulsed, and just as he wretched, another SCSD vehicle whipped by.

Wolf stood up, missing the door handle once with his hand before getting the door open and climbing inside his SUV.

Brief panic hit him as he dug in the wrong pocket for his keys. Then found them in the other. He fired up the SUV, backed out, and drove fast towards town. *Back to the highway.* He decided he needed to get home to regroup.

For a few yards he considered going without lights, but then decided that would be conspicuous and unsafe. There would be more department vehicles driving to the scene.

And how about an SCSD vehicle driving away from the scene? How was that going to look?

Wolf shook his head, took a deep breath, turned on the lights and stepped on it.

"Sheriff Connell is down. I repeat, the sheriff has been shot multiple times."

Wolf turned the radio down and leaned toward the windshield. "Dead on arrival ..." he heard before turning it down. *He needed to think.*

Another set of flashers came around the upcoming bend. He jammed the brakes, swerving and sliding before finally slowing down to a crawl, and pulled to the side of the road.

The approaching department SUV barely slowed in time, but came to a stop at the sight of Wolf's own department SUV going the opposite way.

Wolf was unsure why he stopped, his mind was still fuzzy and slow. But he did know that driving in the opposite direction was going to bring immediate suspicion on him. He needed to buy himself some time.

It stopped next to Wolf's vehicle and lowered its window. Wolf fumbled for the window button and did the same.

Deputy Baine was behind the wheel of the other vehicle, staring wide-eyed and wide-mouthed.

Rachette was next to him with a similar adrenaline-pumped expression. "What's going on?"

Wolf was careful to raise his clean right arm as he pointed back. "Get up there now! Now! I'll be right there!" Wolf drove away fast, checking in the side view mirror.

Baine's brake lights depressed after a few seconds and they drove away into the distance around the bend.

Wolf shook his head and rubbed his face, which felt strangely dry and cracked. He flipped on the cab light and looked in the rearview mirror. The entire left side of his face was painted red with blood, from chin to eyebrow.

"Shit!" He slapped the wheel and turned off the light.

CHAPTER 24

WOLF DROVE at speed the entire way to his ranch, taking side roads through town to avoid further detection. It seemed to be a good move, as he didn't see another department vehicle.

He skidded to a stop in front of the ranch house. He got out and left the headlights on, illuminating the pile of dark rubble that had once been his kitchen, and stumbled through the front door. Inside, he gathered his gear, washed his face in his bedroom bathroom, drinking as much water as he could.

Then he ran to the barn, where he shoved food packets and his camp stove into his backpack. Next, he holstered his Glock into a paddle holster, tucked it into his waist, pocketed some ammo and his Leatherman multi-tool, and uncovered his dirt bike.

Wolf rolled the Yamaha WR450F out through the sliding barn door and leaned it on the kickstand. As it tipped, the gas tank sloshed. He unscrewed the cap and saw that there was a little under a half tank.

He cursed himself for not buying gas as he picked up the empty can on the floor. Then he tossed it and rummaged through the debris field on the workbench to make sure he had all he needed.

He stepped outside and listened to the night. There was a faint hum of a semi downshifting miles away, a few nearby crickets, and a jet flying above.

As he was pulling his helmet on, he heard another faint noise. He yanked it off and held his breath. The sirens had started again, undoubtedly on their way to him.

He put on his helmet and gloves, got on the bike, kicked up the stand, flipped the kick lever out, and prayed.

His prayers were answered as the bike thumped to life on the second kick. Just then, a pair of headlights rose into view, coming up over the ridge through the Bull Horn gate.

Wolf cranked the throttle once, leaned left, almost falling over with a wave of dizziness, and peeled away into the woods.

CHAPTER 25

CONNELL WAS DEAD.

Rachette wasn't afraid to admit that he was relieved. Almost happy even. Who was he kidding? He *was* happy. There was no other way to put it. But worry was starting to take hold over him.

That had been blood all over Wolf's face. There was no mistaking what he and Baine had seen.

The SUV went into a shuddering four-wheel slide around a corner and the back right tire dipped down, then bounced up hard.

"Slow it down, Baine!"

"Shit. Sorry." Baine slowed the pace and looked to Rachette. "You saw his face."

Rachette kept his gaze out through the windshield, half waiting to see a family of deer standing in the middle of the darkened road any second.

"I think we need to call this in." Baine was shooting glances to the road and Rachette like he was watching a tennis match.

"We aren't calling this in. I think Wolf may be in trouble, and we need to go see what's going on. I'm not going to say it again." He glared at Baine. "If you touch your radio, I'll shoot you."

Baine threw back his head. "Geez, man. If he just killed Connell, who knows what kind of condition he's in?" They drove in silence for a little. "You'd better know what you're doing."

"I know Wolf. He's ..."

Baine looked at him. "He's what?"

Rachette spit into his empty Red Bull can and glared out the window. "Just drive."

They rode in silence, following the meandering road next to the Chautauqua, until Wolf's ranch head gate came into view.

The front of the SUV dropped as they drove up to Wolf's property, and the ranch rose into view.

"There he is!" Baine leaned forward, reaching for the radio console.

Rachette grabbed his arm and glared. "Wait a minute. Let's talk to him. Trust me."

Baine ripped his arm back and drove on.

Wolf was fifty yards ahead, a shadow against a beam of light pouring from his barn door. His SUV was parked in the dirt circle driveway, in front of the demolished kitchen.

Rachette squinted and saw that Wolf was sitting on his dirt bike. Wolf kicked twice and a puff of smoke came out the back. Then he jerked his head up and swayed it a little from side to side. It was as if Wolf's helmet was too heavy for his body, or like he was drunk.

Very drunk.

"Stop!" Rachette yelled.

Baine stopped and they got out.

The motorcycle jerked forward with the low sound of a four-stroke engine, and then tipped to the side. Wolf had planted a foot just in time, barely keeping the bike up as it wobbled and lurched forward, all the while the headlight swinging between the side of the house and the trees beyond. Then he spat dirt out from the back tire, rounded the right side of the house, and zipped into the trees out of sight.

They walked to the hood of the Explorer and watched the halogen light flicker through the trees, then come to a dead stop, followed quickly by a loud crack, and then complete silence.

"Holy crap."

Rachette pointed back. "Turn off the engine. Turn it off!"

Baine ran back and shut it off.

They watched quietly as the halogen on Wolf's bike, now halfway up the hill behind Wolf's house, pointed straight up the trunk of a pine tree. The still night carried Wolf's shuffling and grunting from over a hundred yards away, and the bike light righted itself once again. Then the bike roared to life, and zoomed away at psychotic speed, Wolf ripping through the first three gears in a few seconds.

The red taillight bounced out of sight, and the thumping engine finally faded behind the sound of crickets.

"I'm calling." Baine looked to Rachette, ducked in the vehicle, and grabbed the radio.

Rachette didn't protest. The truth was, Rachette didn't know what to think.

CHAPTER 26

BAINE WAS WIDE-EYED and spilling it all to Sergeant Vickers.

"Deputy Rachette and I witnessed Sergeant Wolf proceeding in his vehicle in the opposite direction from Sheriff Connell's. We noticed what looked to be a lot of blood on the side of Sergeant Wolf's face, and he was acting suspicious. So we decided we would follow him to his house. Then we saw—"

Vickers held up a hand and leaned towards Baine. "Blood on the side of Sergeant Wolf's face, son? And you decided to pursue an obvious suspect at that point in complete radio silence? Not calling this in to your fellow deputies, who would be obviously interested in a tidbit of information like this on the night their sheriff had just been shot five times? Murdered? You didn't call this in?"

Rachette stepped forward. "Sir, it was my idea to pursue Sergeant Wolf without calling it in."

"I'm not talkin' to you, son." Vickers spoke slowly, holding up a hand in Rachette's direction.

"I'm not your son, sir." Rachette couldn't help it. The slick hair, each mark of the comb grooved into his head, the perfect five o'clock shadow, the unisex cologne slathered on his skin, the silky condescending voice that commanded ultimate respect, not one iota of it deserved, the way he entered a room and asked, *How we doing?* We? He couldn't stand Sergeant Vickers. Or was it *Sheriff* Vickers now?

Vickers turned and looked at Rachette, holding his expressionless gaze for what seemed like a full minute, and then turned back to Baine.

Rachette walked away through the group of lurking deputies and approached what looked to be Wilson's vehicle driving up the road.

Deputy Wilson teetered out of his SUV and walked over, adjusting his pants like he always did, apparently not liking the tight fit on his ample frame. His partner, Hayburn, wasn't far behind, out the passenger door.

"What the heck's going on?" Wilson was a fellow second year. His pupils were wide open, and he didn't blink. It was the second time in two days that the full roster of deputies had convened on Wolf's property, and just like the first time, everyone was jacked up.

"I don't know." Rachette wasn't going to speculate. There was no denying it, though. It wasn't looking too good. Wolf's blood had been found on the accelerator, brake pedal, and floor mat of his SUV. Boot prints were found trudging through Connell's blood at the murder scene. There were five shell casings found at the scene. It would be a simple matter to match any fingerprints on the casings to Wolf's.

He didn't like it one bit. But Wolf could still be innocent. Or if he was guilty, he would have had a good reason to do what he did.

Shit. There wasn't a good reason for murder like that.

Everyone turned toward the gate as a roaring diesel engine and pair of headlights rose into view.

Rachette perked up as Vickers stopped talking to Baine and

walked towards the approaching lights. He was straightening his shirt and adjusting his belt, waiting with a solemn expression.

As the large Ford diesel truck thundered closer, Rachette could see the double-horseshoe symbol painted on the door.

Gary Connell cut the engine and stepped out of the truck, or more like fell out of it, stumbling onto his knees, then got up and marched to Vickers. "Where the fuck is he?"

Vickers took off his hat and said some low words that Rachette couldn't hear, pointed towards the barn, then the hills beyond the half-charred house.

Gary Connell was a mess. His eyes were bloodshot and streaming, and his upper lip was shiny with snot. He wiped both on the long sleeve of his flannel pajama top and walked alongside Vickers.

Rachette noticed that Gary Connell still had slippers on and he felt a twang of pity for the man. Rachette had not had many interactions with Gary Connell over the couple years he had been in town. In fact, Gary hadn't said a single word to Rachette other than *Nice to meet you* as they shook hands at some point during the previous summer.

The man's attitude emanated a power and confidence he hadn't seen in anyone else but Wolf. And for sixty or so years old, he was in impressive physical shape. Put it all together—the man, the money, and the power—and he was an imposing figure, to say the least. So when Gary locked his wide eyes on Rachette's, pointed, and marched straight towards him, Rachette's pulse raised a few BPMs.

"You're Rachette?" He didn't wait for an answer. "Why didn't you call this in earlier?"

Rachette sucked in a breath and set his feet, wondering whether he was about to get strangled for the second time in less than eight hours. This time by Dad.

"Sir. We—I didn't think that—"

Gary waved a hand. "We don't have any time to listen to your bullshit answer." His voice quivered as his eyes bore into Rachette's. "I know who you are, and how you'd do anything to protect Wolf." He stepped close and finger-pecked Rachette's chest. "Just know this, Rachette, if anything else goes wrong from now on, you're out of a job. I'll see to it personally."

Rachette nodded and noticed Wilson shuffling into the quiet obscurity of the rest of the men.

To Rachette's relief, Gary turned and walked on, raising his voice to address the group.

"Sergeant David Wolf killed my only son tonight. Shot him five times." His head dropped and his body shook, sobbing. "Where did he go?"

Gary stared at the ground for a few seconds, then looked sideways and lifted his head. "That was a question! Where did he go?"

Rachette cleared his throat. "Sir, he was on his—"

"Not you." Gary's voice was ice as he pointed a shaking finger at Rachette.

Baine spoke up. "Sir, when we arrived, we witnessed him get on his motorcycle. He had a backpack on, and was dressed in black. He went up the hill around the back of the house. He looked intoxicated, I think. We witnessed him crash the motorcycle into a tree, then he picked up the bike and continued around the mountain on that trail." Baine pointed. "That trail up there."

Gary narrowed his eyes, looking to the moonlit mountain covered with burned, skeletal trees. "This is a dangerous man, Deputies. Five shots, two to the head, three to the body." His voice was steady as he stared into nothing. "That's what he did to my son."

He paced in front of the deputies, looking at the ground, then stopped. "I just want to remind you men that David Wolf is an ex-army ranger. A trained killing machine. Don't be fooled for one second. The man you have gotten to know over the past few years is gone. The smiling face, the friendship you may have garnered with him over the years." He looked pointedly to Rachette. "That is long gone. You saw what he did to my son last week, and now he's finished the job." He shook his head. "He's snapped."

The men surrounding Rachette glanced at one another. They were shaking their heads, looking like they disbelieved how far one of their own had fallen.

What he did to my son last week? Were they really believing this?

Gary looked to Vickers and nodded.

Vickers took the silent cue and stepped forward. "There's more, guys. We've got a positive match on fingerprints taken from the knife found at the stabbing last night. They're Wolf's."

Rachette's stomach twisted.

"Deputy Rachette, can you tell us all who Mark Wilson is?" Vickers asked.

"Uh ... excuse me?"

"I asked you, can you please tell us who Mark Wilson is, Deputy Rachette?"

"I've ... I've never met him, sir."

"I didn't ask that. Can you tell us who he is, please?"

Gary was glaring at Rachette with a snarl on his face.

Vickers held his determined stare.

"Mark Wilson is now lying in a critical condition in County General," Vickers said. "And who do you think is there to comfort him as he sits on the brink of death? His girlfriend, Sarah Muller. Formerly known as Sarah Wolf." Vickers let his glare linger on Rachette for a few more seconds, and then turned to the others.

"We have a killer on the loose. He's stabbed his ex-wife's

boyfriend, and now he's killed our sheriff. We need to stop this man before he kills again.

"I have K-9 units on the way from Summit County, and we'll have a chopper at our disposal tomorrow morning. Right now, I want every deputy down at the station in fifteen for a briefing."

"If I may say something here, Sergeant Vickers." Gary sniffed and wiped his eyes, stepping forward.

"Of course, sir."

"I think he may be coming after me. He called me yesterday, after this happened," he pointed to the charred remains of the ranch-house kitchen, "on Derek's phone. I don't know, you guys might have seen it. He seemed pretty angry. Then I heard that fight break out from over the phone." He breathed a heavy sigh. "I don't know why, but I just think it may be a good idea to check the trails that lead north to my ranch. Or any of the trails behind the ranch as well. He's out for blood. And I have a feeling his sights are on me."

Rachette studied Gary. Was Gary behind the explosion yesterday? Was Wolf right? Rachette looked at the tinted windows of Gary's Ford truck. Was that big ex-navy SEAL that Wolf was talking about in there?

"Thank you, sir." Vickers finger-combed his stiff hair and bowed his head. "We'll find him, sir. Words cannot express how sorry we are for your loss."

Gary sniffed, looked to the stars as a tear streamed down his cheek, and then walked to his truck.

"All right! Let's get going!" Vickers twirled his hand above his head and the men scrambled to their vehicles.

The front of Wolf's property exploded into the sound of engines firing, lights bathing the grass and surrounding trees. Over it all, Rachette heard Gary's diesel roar to life as it reversed into the field. For a moment, its headlights stopped on Rachette.

Rachette stood still, squinting into the blinding beams.

"Rachette, let's go!" Baine's voice was barely audible over the erupting engines.

Rachette stood unmoved.

The diesel rolled slowly forward for a few feet, like a bull beginning a charge. Then the front wheels turned and it thundered down the way it had come.

CHAPTER 27

GARY WATCHED Buck scale the side of the large excavator and shove his head into the open compartment that exposed the inner workings of the machine. Slivers of light escaped from the engine housing as he dug around with his flashlight. Then he jumped down and went to the rear, opened another compartment, and put on the screw cap.

When he was done, Buck climbed into the cab and fired it up.

The excavator jumped from the torque of the roaring engine and spewed a cloud of smoke from the exhaust.

And right there was the reason he kept Buck around.

Earl was high on the hill keeping watch—a less impressive, but just as vital role.

The boom raised, the stick extended, and the bucket dug in high on the scree pile and then pulled down. He lifted a pile of the big rocks, twisted the cab, and dropped them to the ground with a thud that Gary could feel in his feet.

Gary took a Cohiba Behike out of his pocket, cut it, and lit it with a wooden match. He only ever smoked the ultra-expensive brand of cigar on occasions when he'd accomplished a major feat, completed tasks that had particularly drained him such as a successful bear kill with a bow, a lucrative land deal, or a profitable merger. Whatever the occasion, in order to smoke one of these, it had to be an incredibly difficult task that took all his skills and pushed him to the limits of his will power and determination.

He puffed gently, walking away from the deafening diesel, rolling the soft cylinder between his fingers, knowing he'd earned every molecule of the fragrant smoke that streamed out of his nostrils.

Gary sucked in the delicious vapor and narrowed his eyes, watching Buck shovel rocks in the distance.

Sure, Young had pulled the trigger and done the dirty work, but Gary's acting job in front of the men of the sheriff's department had been a thing of beauty to top it all off. And that was putting it mildly. That performance was a final act of an entire life's work. Looking at it that way, he deserved more than this four-hundred-and-fifty-dollar rolled-up piece of junk for what he had just endured.

And what he had just endured was playing a part for the past twenty-five years. *Had it been that long?* Had it been twenty-five years since he had learned that that muscle-bound weak excuse for a human being was not even his own son?

His wife had paid immediately for the lie. And ever since her untimely death, he had been paying for it a thousand fold.

For twenty-five years he'd been putting on the act of his life, pretending to care about that worthless sack of muscles in order to deflect any suspicion of his involvement in Derek's mother's death. Well, he was finally done paying. It was like selling off a toxic asset. No more pretending.

He relaxed his grip on the Cohiba and puffed it gently again.

A husky voice warmed his ear. "Gotcha."

Gary turned, flipping the cigar out of his mouth and onto the ground in a shower of sparks. "Shit! Don't do that!"

Young stood back and stared towards the excavator.

Gary was beginning to think there was something supernatural about this guy. "Did you drive here? Where's your car?"

"It's down the road."

Gary eyed him as Earl's voice scratched through the radio. "You okay, boss?"

"Yeah, yeah." Gary put the radio back on his belt, picked up the cigar with a quick brush and lit it again. Young was smiling at him. "What?"

"Nothing." Young was studying him with a slight look of ... was it respect? "I just didn't think you'd be so ... normal. You know, after your son was so brutally murdered tonight and all."

"He wasn't my son." Gary's voice was almost inaudible. He puffed a few times and flipped ash onto the ground.

Young raised his eyebrows.

They stood in silence, watching Buck work the machinery.

"So?" Gary gave him a sideways glance and held out his hand.

"So what?"

He turned to Young. "What do you mean, so what? Where is it?"

Young smiled again. "Relax. He didn't have it on him. It's probably at his house. I obviously couldn't get it last night." His eyes bore into Gary's. "I'll get it."

"Shit." Gary put the cigar in his mouth. "What about Wolf?"

Young's eyes were half closed. "He's headed towards us, just like we thought. He stopped about halfway, probably to pass out for the night. I'm heading to your house now to get some rest, then I'll get him in the morning."

Gary glared at Young. "I'm telling you, this guy isn't a

pushover. You'll have to watch your ass with him now. He knows you're coming."

Young's face didn't move a millimeter. Did he even breathe?

"Pretty slow going," Young finally said, nodding towards the excavator.

"Well, good thing you have plenty else to worry about besides what goes on here."

Young stared at Gary. "Oh, I'm not worried about what happens here one bit."

A chill crawled up Gary's spine as he thought about that. "If this doesn't work out, you'll be out of a job, for one."

"And that's all I'll be. Out of a job." Young slapped Gary on the shoulder, hard, then turned to walk through the gate.

CHAPTER 28

WOLF CROUCHED in a hole on a bare mountainside high above treeline. At over twelve thousand feet, it was still well below freezing in the shaded southwestern slope. Just a few feet away, the eastern side of the mountain was bathed in the warmth of the rising sun. But he didn't want to risk any reflections so he kept inside the shadow.

He tucked his chin underneath the neck of his frosty jacket, and with as little movement as possible scanned the terrain below through his high-powered binoculars.

It had been an hour since the first rays of light had risen over the eastern peaks, and Wolf could now see shimmering pinpoint reflections off windows and rooftops in town far below to the west.

There didn't seem to be any action out of the ordinary in town—not that he could see much from such a distance—but he knew the manhunt would be well underway by now.

Wolf sat up a little as he heard a faint rumble of a four-stroke engine. It sounded like a motorcycle—like his Yamaha or an ATV. It grew louder below, and finally he could sense it was coming from the right.

He pointed the binoculars as a four-wheeler slowly came over the hill and stopped. Its engine at an idle was almost inaudible from the four-hundred-yard distance.

The image of Young on a parked ATV bounced gently in Wolf's binoculars. The big guy was digging for something in a pack on his lap, looking down. Then he unshouldered his rifle and pointed it towards the group of bushes where Wolf had ditched the motorcycle.

Wolf narrowed his eyes.

Young seemed to think better of taking the shot, and shouldered his rifle, then accelerated fast down the hill.

Wolf followed with the lenses.

A few seconds later the sound waves of the thumping engine hit—a long sustained acceleration that ended in scraping tires.

Young jumped off and walked to the lone clump of foliage on an otherwise desolate-looking high-mountain landscape.

There was no way he could have seen the bike from the top of the hill, or could see it at all now. Wolf had made sure of that the night before.

Wolf had ridden hard for over three hours, leaving scent decoys, doubling back on his trail numerous times, ultimately ending up in a place that was as nondescript as any.

He was nowhere near Gary's 2Shoe ranch, miles away in fact, and he'd hidden the bike completely. Nonetheless, here was Young. And Young walked straight to it, bent down, and threw back the limbs Wolf had placed over it without a second's hesitation.

Soon it made sense. Young dug around for a few seconds, as if looking for something on the bike, or underneath it. When he stood up, he had a small white object in his hand. He pulled another item from his pocket and looked at them both, then walked to his four-wheeler and dug in the pack on the back of his seat.

He had retrieved a GPS tracking device.

Wolf began taking mental stock of all the gear he'd taken from his house the previous night, all the while keeping the big man in the bobbing view of his binoculars. Wolf was reasonably confident that there were no more devices on him. More likely, Young had attached them to Wolf's vehicles, keeping track of him all last night, and then getting an early start this morning.

Wolf swung the binoculars back to the crest of the hill where Young had come from. There was nobody else. Certainly not any cops. Wolf cursed himself for not bringing a rifle.

Young was obviously out for blood, and at this point he would be praised as a hero if he came back with Wolf's head in a duffle bag. He was alone, so he could say it was self-defense if he killed Wolf. Or maybe there were strict shoot-to-kill orders for Wolf right now straight from Vickers, the acting sheriff.

Wolf shivered. Not because he was still covered with overnight frost, but at the thought that Gary Connell had murdered his only son. Why? To create this chance to kill Wolf?

Or had he? Maybe this Young guy was working alone with his own agenda. If so, why?

Wolf swept the binoculars back downhill.

His stomach lurched as the distant image filled his view. Young was standing dead still, pointing his rifle straight at him.

Wolf held his breath and didn't blink. Every muscle on his body tensed, ready to duck at the first sign of a muzzle flash, knowing that the bullet could reach him faster than the sound of the shot.

After a few agonizing moments, Young slowly swung his rifle to the shadowed slope to Wolf's right, then back and forth a few times.

Wolf stayed still, taking slow breaths into the neck of his coat, hoping his breath was invisible at such a distance.

With a lightning-quick movement, Young put the rifle on his shoulder, then crouched down, feeling the ground with his hand.

In just a few seconds, Young found Wolf's tracks and followed them.

Wolf relaxed as Young walked in the opposite direction, following the misdirection Wolf had laid down. His tracks went on for hundreds of yards and would end on a flat granite formation in the distance. Even so, Wolf had continued for another hundred yards, leaving telltale scrapes in lichen and overturned pebbles before doubling back and finally resting in his current spot.

After twenty yards, Young stood straight, turned around, marched back towards his four-wheeler, and fired it up.

Wolf watched for twenty minutes as Young crept up the open expanse, following Wolf's tracks, leaning off the edge of his seat.

At the summit of the gentle rise, Young paused, scanning in front of him, then disappeared over the hill. The droning engine faded to nothing a few seconds later.

Wolf pulled out his cell phone. It had no service, and the battery was almost dead. He pulled out his Leatherman multi-tool, wrenched off the SIM cardholder, and removed the card.

He pressed the power button, then, with a sharp breath, remembered the attempted audio recording from last night, and switched the phone back on.

Dammit. The drug hangover slowed his mind, and was beginning to get on his nerves.

He opened the voice-memo application and looked at the

latest file. It was thirty-seven minutes long, dated the night before. He pushed play.

Wolf stretched his legs, scanned the horizon of where Young had just gone, and listened.

"Gotcha." It was the whisper in his ear. *On* his ear. It seemed a lot louder on the recording than he remembered. It was more of a loud declaration by Young than the whisper Wolf remembered. Then there was a full five minutes of shuffling, scraping, grunting, and inaudible noises from Young.

Then five blasts.

And a lot of laughing.

Wolf narrowed his eyes and listened to the phone—another few minutes of shuffling, all the while with the same incessant laughing. Wolf turned up the volume as loud as it would go.

Young's voice was muffled and sounded distant. "Oh, you're dead now. You're dead now. You're dead now." Then there was a long pause. "You dead?"

Wolf put the speaker to his ear.

It sounded like Young was hyperventilating. Then came a series of maniacal giggles, each one rising in pitch as if asking a question.

Wolf looked at the phone, a chill snaking up his body.

The guy was a nut-job. He'd seen men in the army who seemed to enjoy killing too much. But this was taking it to a whole new level.

Maybe Young *was* acting alone.

Wolf put the speaker back to his ear. There was dead silence.

He pressed his finger on the forward button, stopping at a sound. He reversed and played it.

It sounded like Young was making a phone call, with a lot of back-and-forth talking in a calm manner.

The call ended, and there were several minutes of silence again.

Wolf pressed his finger on the forward button, waiting for another sign of sounds.

He stopped and reversed again near the end. It was Young trying to wake him up, throwing water and smacking him.

"Hi, I just heard shots fired at Derek Connell's place. There were a lot of them. Please come quick ... Wake up, you've only got a few minutes."

Then there was the sound of Wolf missing two calls, him slowly snapping out of his unconscious state, and his drunken words with Rachette.

Wolf stopped the recording, shut off the phone completely, and took a deep breath.

There was no reason for Young to have let Wolf go, to have warned him that the cops were coming, unless Young had wanted him to run—to be in the situation he found himself in now.

And right now? Wolf was a dangerous man who had just shot the sheriff five times, and then fled into the woods. He was a hunted man.

Shoot to kill. Wolf knew with a sinking feeling that those would be the orders.

Wolf stood up on legs that ached from a long night's ride, chock full of uncirculated lactic acid from sitting still for hours on end in the freezing temperature.

He looked again to the horizon and listened to the chirps of marmots scurrying above him, squinted into the warmth of the rising sun, found the rocky formation he was looking for, took two quick breaths, and began jogging.

CHAPTER 29

YOUNG DROVE SLOWLY over the gentle rise, and then accelerated hard downhill for fifty yards. He slammed the brakes, skidding the ATV to a ninety-degree stop, and killed the engine at the same time. Before it came to rest, he jumped off on the downhill side and landed, his feet already moving as fast as they could.

Young sprinted downhill, reaching the tree line, then hopped over a fallen tree at breakneck speed, landed on the knife-edge of a boulder, stepped onto a flat rock, and jumped.

Thirty feet later he landed on a steep dirt chute in a feet-first baseball slide. Just before careening into a car-sized rock, he dug in his boots and jumped, hand-slap-vaulting over it with ease. He ran to his left and jumped onto a steep scree pile.

The wind rushed through his closely cropped hair as he took giant, bouncing strides straight down the loose rock. He gained even more speed, covering huge distances with each step, until he turned at just the right moment, executing a long hockey stop.

In a fluid move, he stepped onto a narrow dirt trail, and looked up with a lazy expression. He'd covered the hundreds of vertical feet in seconds. Maybe he'd take up extreme skiing this upcoming winter.

He squinted and saw the gleam of the red four-wheeler on the slope above. If someone saw it, they saw it. It didn't matter. He'd left no trace of himself on it. He never did.

He began jogging.

His lips curled into a small smile as he thought about Wolf, sitting on the side of the hill, then he frowned. Wolf's mistake was almost disappointing. But the whole interaction had made it interesting at least.

Does he see me? Is he gonna shoot?

He allowed a small laugh, then blanked his face and upped the pace.

CHAPTER 30

WOLF PUSHED HARD up the side of the mountain, cursing the cigarettes he'd allowed himself the past two weeks as a searing pain developed in the center of his lungs. His legs weren't in the kind of shape he would have liked either—his calves were knots, his thighs sluggish, and a strain had opened up in the right side of his groin. His mind, however, pushed him forward without mercy.

He didn't know whether he was being paranoid, but the more Wolf had thought about Young, staring at him through the rifle scope, the faster Wolf had run, until finally Wolf had been in an all-out sprint for ten minutes—fighting for the high ground he scaled towards now.

When he reached the top of the rise, he stopped, keeping a rock outcropping to the west, towards the way he'd just come from. He huffed through his teeth for a minute, then finally closed his mouth, fighting the coughing reflex the best he could. *Damn cigarettes.*

Wolf's thumping heart was loud in his ears as he leaned against the rock and peered over the side.

Not thirty seconds later he heard a noise.

Young came into view from behind a rock outcropping far below and to the left. His feet pounded on the dusty trail in a fast perfect rhythm. His huge strides propelled his body forward with the ferocity of a charging grizzly bear. His face, however, was dead calm, as if watching a boring TV show.

He covered fifty yards with the speed of an NFL wide receiver, then slowed to a dead stop just below Wolf with an agility that didn't seem natural for such a large man.

He looked up the slope opposite Wolf and pumped his lungs with big heaves of his chest. After a full minute of standing still and catching his breath, he turned in a slow circle. *Listening.*

Wolf's lungs itched and rattled, demanding he expel the cigarette tar with a violent cough. He smothered his face in his sleeve and breathed slow.

Young did a full circle and then looked down. He was scanning the dusty trail for prints.

Wolf had crossed the trail no more than fifty feet beyond where Young was. If it came down to it, and Young came up after him, Wolf would be able to sit tight and pick him off from his higher ground. Of course, Young would know that. Picking Young off now would take out any uncertainty, but he was too far to hit with his Glock.

Finally, it looked like Young had come to a decision, snapping his head up the slope to the west.

Wolf watched the big man climb with ease, gaining altitude fast, all the while following parallel with Wolf's tracks.

Thankfully Young kept meandering his way left, away from the tracks, and finally climbed out of view, undoubtedly to ambush Wolf where he had sat fifteen minutes ago.

Wolf inhaled and muffled a hard cough into his sleeve, clearing his lungs in one push. There was no telling how long it would take Young to realize that Wolf was gone, and then to figure out just where to. Wolf was counting on Young thinking he'd gone north and west, towards the two peaks—towards the backside of Connell's ranch.

If Young was an experienced tracker, however, he might see what little ground sign Wolf had left, leading him back down the way he'd come, and hot on Wolf's trail to the east.

He'd bought some time. But how much?

He turned to the northeast and picked out the dark-brown cone of rock. It was miles away on the other side of the vast forested valley floor. The journey would provide good cover, the prize at the end hopefully being help. Maybe even a rifle.

But it had been a long time. Would the old guy recognize him? Was he even alive? Would he shoot Wolf?

There was no better option.

CHAPTER 31

RACHETTE CRUNCHED his way over the dried pine needles and stepped over a log, scratching his ankle on a jagged branch. "Shit."

Vickers stopped, shooting him a glare over his shoulder. He'd been watching Rachette like a hawk since they left Wolf's property at first light. Vickers was obviously certain that Rachette was going to be in touch with Wolf at some point, and Vickers was determined to catch him in the act.

It was getting old.

"Not talking to Wolf." Rachette raised his hands.

Vickers stared at him a beat, then turned around and kept walking.

After a few minutes, a deputy led by a hulking German shepherd came scrambling into view straight ahead of them. "It's another scent decoy." The K-9 unit deputy from Summit County held up a dirty sock stuffed with rocks towards Vickers.

Rachette suppressed a smile.

"This is getting ridiculous. Do we even have the general direction he went in?" Vickers took off his cowboy hat, wiped his forehead, and looked into the distance.

They had been moving north with the dogs, which had been following Wolf's scent for the past hour. Before that, they'd headed southeast for an hour and a half. The net effect on their location was somewhere straight east of Wolf's ranch, on the sunbaked side of a thinly treed mountain.

It was hot, Rachette's body was aching, and he was desperate for sleep. Then Rachette thought of Wolf. With the misdirection the search teams were encountering, he doubted Wolf had had any sleep the night before.

Rachette pulled his phone from his pocket and gave it a quick look again. There was no sign of a message from Wolf.

Vickers saw him do it, and Rachette didn't care.

The helicopter thumped over the ridge into view again, drowning out any sounds.

Vickers watched the helicopter leave and fade into the distance as he walked over. He took off his backpack and set it on the ground, took a sip of his water, and held it out to Rachette.

Rachette shook his head.

"What do you think?" Vickers wafted his shirt. The smell of cologne and sweat billowed out in an invisible noxious cloud.

"What do you mean?"

Vickers looked at Rachette. "You know Wolf. Tell me what you're thinking. You keep checking that phone."

Rachette narrowed his eyes. It was the first time Vickers had given him a sincere look in the eye since they had met. Like they were suddenly equals. "I think he didn't do any of this."

Vickers gave a high-pitched laugh, closing his eyes to the sky. "Come on. Seriously?"

Rachette said nothing.

Vickers held up a hand. "Okay, fine. But you've gotta convince me here. You think your man didn't do this. Why? Tell me."

Rachette held the man's gaze. "Who the hell are you?"

Vickers blinked. "What do you mean?"

"You heard me. You come waltzing in here, and take Wolf's position while Connell takes sheriff?"

"I was hired by Sluice County, just like you."

Rachette shook his head and gave a laugh of his own. "Nah. Not just like me. You had a straight line into the Sheriff's Department through the Connells. I came in here and interviewed for the job with the sheriff, just like everyone else in this department. I never saw you set foot in the station until the day you started. How'd you pull that off?"

Vickers glared. "I was recruited by Mr. Connell, hired by the county council." His voice turned icy. "And that's that."

Rachette shook his head and looked down the slope.

Vickers took another sip of water. "Look, I'm serious here. I want to know how you think Wolf could not be responsible for murder. If not him, then who?"

Rachette wondered just what angle Vickers was taking. Was he reporting back to Gary?

"Fine. Keep quiet." Vickers put his bottle in his backpack, shouldered it, and walked away. After a few feet, he came to a halt. "I keep hearing about how great this guy Wolf is. The truth is, I'd sure like to believe the great stories, and I'd sure like to work with a guy like that if I'm going to live out my career in the Sluice County Sheriff's Department, which I plan on doing. I, for one, like it here. Just like I know you do." He kept walking.

"Sergeant Vickers."

Vickers stopped and turned his head halfway.

Rachette took a sip of his water and decided it couldn't hurt to talk. "Tuesday night at the Beer Goggles Bar, Wolf was sure he saw a needle mark on Jerry Blackman's neck. Was there? Were there drugs in his system?"

Vickers turned around and nodded. "We found some sedatives in his system."

"Why would Wolf do that to the guy? Secondly, Wolf pointed that out to me. Why would he point out the needle mark on Blackman's neck? And Wolf also found some large footprints and tire tread marks that led to the back of the bar. It looked like someone, a very large someone, had backed a truck up and unloaded Mark Wilson's body."

"Why didn't Wolf mention any of this to us?" Vickers asked.

"I don't know, maybe because earlier that day his house had exploded. Almost killing his son in the process. And he had all the reason in the world to believe Connell was behind that. He saw a flash inside the door, and he was suspecting arson, which was confirmed by the fire investigators, by the way. So why would he go telling his theories to Connell? And who's to say *you* didn't know about the explosion, too?"

Vickers stared for a few long seconds and raised his eyebrows. "Did you know that Gary was going to raise the rent on Wolf's property?"

Rachette frowned at the sudden shift in topics. And, no, he hadn't known about that.

Vickers softened his expression. "From what I've gathered from Gary, Wolf was pretty furious about not getting the sheriff job and threatened Gary after he tried to offer Wolf a job. Gary reacted a little harshly, telling him he was going to have to raise the rent, which he says he had no intention of doing." Vickers shrugged. "So, the question is, what if Wolf rigged the house to blow? Out of revenge or spite." Vickers stepped closer and cocked his head. "Didn't Wolf's father build that house? And now he was getting run out by Gary?"

Rachette shook his head. "No. Listen." Rachette looked vacantly at the approaching helicopter. "What about the big ex-navy SEAL guy Gary is hanging out with? The chief of security for the mining company, or whatever he is. Young, that's his name. Those were *Young's* boot prints at the stabbing. Young drugged Mark Wilson and Jerry Blackman out back of the Beer Goggles Bar, and then planted the knife on Blackman."

Vickers dropped his gaze and scraped the dirt with his boot. He looked up and shrugged. "Who's Young?"

Rachette looked away as he felt his face flush. Rachette realized he'd never actually seen the ex-navy SEAL in question.

Vickers nodded. "I know it must be hard to see your mentor unraveling in front of your eyes." He held up his hands quickly. "Or maybe he just didn't do any of this, like you said. But let's look at what the facts are telling us. He just came back from a harrowing experience, bringing his dead brother back from overseas. His ex-wife just gets out of rehab, and she's dating some other guy instead of him. And to top it off, he doesn't get appointed to sheriff, a job he wanted more than anything in the world. A job his father used to have before he was killed in the line of duty. Hell," Vickers ripped off his hat, slapped it on his leg, and squinted into the sun, "I'd snap if I was him, too. Sure as *shit* I'd snap."

Rachette's mind swirled as he looked into the trees below. *Connell.* He'd seen the murderous intent in Connell's eyes as he'd strangled Rachette against the garage wall.

Rachette nodded and stepped forward. "All right. We'll see."

Vickers put a firm hand on his shoulder. "We'll shoot first, and then we'll see." His eyebrows were raised high. "I'm in charge now, and that's an order. I'm not going to jeopardize more lives on your defiant hunch. You got that, Deputy Rachette?"

Rachette ducked his shoulder and walked away.

CHAPTER 32

SWEAT SLID down the side of Wolf's cheek as he walked on the fine rocky soil of the valley floor. He stopped in the trees near the edge of a clearing, wiped his forehead with his bare forearm and pulled his wet camo tee shirt away from his skin.

It was humid, and dark clouds were popping straight up into tall towers in the southwest.

The cone of rock he'd known as Pyramid Peak—a steep geological formation hundreds of feet high, with no trees, and millions of years old—was close now, looming high above the pines just to the north.

He took off his backpack and crammed a nutrition bar in his mouth, then took a quick gulp of water and stood still in the freshening breeze. Wolf could smell the strange aftershave-like scent again, this time closer.

He stood dead still. "It's David Wolf. I'm here to see you."

There was no sound except the wind breathing through the tops of the trees, and the long chattering of a treetop squirrel.

Wolf set down the water and held out both his arms, palms out.

The voice came from behind him. "Turn around slow."

Wolf did.

The first thing he saw was the muzzle of a rifle. The wood stock of it was tucked into the armpit of a dirty brown tee shirt, like how a little kid would hold a toy rifle. But the man holding the gun wasn't playing. The hammer was cocked, his finger was white on the trigger, and the muzzle was still.

Wolf spoke quickly. "Sir, it's David Wolf. Do you remember me? I've been here a couple times with my father, Daniel Wolf."

The old man's eyes narrowed and he looked Wolf up and down. "David Wolf?"

A waft of breeze hit them, bringing with it the faint thumping sound of the helicopter circling the sky to the southwest.

The pulsing of the rotor grew louder and the man tilted his head and gave it a glance.

Wolf didn't move. He didn't need to look. From the sound, he knew it was searching near the ditched motorcycle, miles away. Instead, he studied the familiar man before him.

It had been seventeen years since he last saw Martin Running Warrior. The old man's skin was rougher now, looking like deeply tanned, well-worn leather. His eyes were dark coffee, wide and alert. Straight silver hair, wet with sweat around his ears, peeked out from underneath a dusty gray cowboy hat that had a band of turquoise beads around the crown.

Wolf remembered the rifle from seventeen years ago—a Winchester with engraved silver plating where the shoulder stock met the barrel. It looked well cleaned and oiled.

Martin flicked a glance towards the helicopter as the sound faded, then tilted his head again. "What's my Navajo name?"

"I don't remember." Wolf watched him narrow his eyes. "I just remember what it means. Running Warrior."

The man relaxed and lowered his rifle, then uncocked the

hammer, shaking his head. "It's Hashké Dilwo'ii" He leaned forward, emphasizing the syllables.

Wolf nodded.

Martin scoffed and glared at him. "There is nothing worse than forgetting who you are." He turned and began walking toward Pyramid Peak. "I take it you aren't here for a refresher course." He gestured in the direction of the faint drone of the helicopter. "I take it you are looking for a place to hide."

Wolf followed close. "I need help, and I need to use your phone. I'm in a bit of trouble."

Martin stopped and looked him up and down for a second. "You look just like your father."

Wolf nodded, unsure how to respond.

Martin's house was a large shoebox design made from decaying wood. The corrugated metal roof was pieced together from smaller scraps of all shapes, sizes, and rust hues. No perimeter fencing or landscaping surrounded the house, but heaps of old tools, machines, and bones seemed to clearly mark where Martin had decided his property ended and nature began.

Behind the house was a tall outcropping of granite and, beyond that, the towering Pyramid Peak cinder cone.

There were no roads entering the property, and Martin looked like he still didn't have a car, but there was an ATV under a tree, covered by a tarp.

Wolf wondered how many visitors Martin had on his property per year. Probably countable on one hand.

Martin led him inside the small building, sat him in a chair, and slapped down a steaming plastic plate of dark-brown meat stew piled on top of potatoes.

Wolf sat motionless at the tiny kitchen table, his mouth

watering at the aroma of the food in front of him. He hesitated, eyeing Martin's empty hands.

"Eat. I've got plenty more." Martin opened a small refrigerator that sat on a flaking linoleum floor, pulled out one of many Tupperware containers, and poured some of the contents into a pot on the gas stove. "I was making lunch when I heard you coming."

Wolf raised an eyebrow and dug into the stew, wondering how the man could have been cooking inside his cabin and yet heard his approach. Wolf recognized the gamey taste of elk as he chewed. The broth was filled with spices, the potatoes soft. It was heaven in a spoon.

Martin turned on the stove and stirred the contents of the pot.

The rectangular space of the room was adorned with various Navajo works of art. The obvious attention to interior decoration lay in stark contrast to the utilitarian junk-pile look of the exterior. A cast-iron wood stove was the centerpiece of the tiny house. A cot topped with folded blankets of Navajo design squatted in one corner, and a bookshelf adorned with stacks of books stood in another. It looked to be filled exclusively with survival and Native American publications.

Wolf felt self-conscious in the presence of the man. Other than knowing that he himself was one-eighth Navajo—Wolf's great-grandfather being full-blooded—his knowledge of the Navajo Nation was limited. Years ago his father had brought him to Martin a few times for that very reason: to teach him about his heritage.

Since then, he'd forgotten most of what he'd learned. He realized that there was another reason for wearing the ring he'd found on his father's armoire. Guilt. Wearing the ring felt like he was keeping the connection. But, he knew, wearing the ring was an action that didn't take any real commitment on his part.

Wolf's stomach sank as he thumbed his left pinky, realizing his father's ring was gone.

He tried to think back to when he'd had it on last. He must have pulled it off when he removed his gloves one of the many times last night. Which meant it could have been anywhere in the hundreds of square miles of forest to the south.

"What's wrong?" Martin sat down and took a spoon-full from his bowl.

Wolf rubbed his finger. "I uh ... lost my father's ring." He picked up his spoon and took a bite.

"Important to you, was it?" Martin asked.

Wolf nodded. "It was actually a Navajo design."

"Really? Silver, was it?"

"Yeah. It was." Wolf glanced at him. "Why?"

"It was probably made by the Atsidii." He pointed through the wall to the north, waited, and then rolled his eyes. "The Silversmith."

Wolf shrugged. "I'm not sure."

Martin got up and went to his bookshelf, then returned with a bracelet. He held it in front of Wolf's face. "Did it have this marking?" He pointed to a square engraving on the inside of the bracelet. "This was his mark."

Wolf reached out and rubbed the mark. "Yes. It did have that. And it had another engraving."

"What did it say?"

Wolf squirmed in his chair. "I don't remember the Navajo words. But I know it meant 'I Love You.' Then there was a year —1985."

Martin stared at him a beat. "Ayóó' ánííníshní. That is what the engraving said, if it said I love you."

Wolf kept eating. "You said, *was* the Silversmith's mark. Is the Silversmith dead?"

Martin swallowed a mouthful of food, then raised a lip like

he was a snarling dog. "No. The Silversmith lived here many years ago, then sold his land and left with his family." He said it with such contempt that it looked like he might spit on the table.

Wolf straightened. "You seem upset about it."

Martin ate a few bites, breathing heavily through his nose. "He sold the land to the mining company, so they could rape it." He glared at Wolf.

"The Connell-Brack Mine to the north?" Wolf raised his eyebrows. "He owned all that land?"

Martin shook his head. "Not *that* land. He sold *his* land. To the south."

"Are you talking about the land just east of the highway? East of Cave Creek Canyon, with the old run-down house on it?" He thought about his conversation with Dennis Muller.

Martin continued eating. "Yes. That is the land."

"But there are no tailings. No mine entrances, no pits. That land is untouched except for that old house."

Martin pointed with his fork. "You don't see it, but they are raping the land from underneath. I wouldn't be surprised if the entire mountainside collapsed today."

Wolf narrowed his eyes and took another bite.

Martin continued eating with his head down. "They will come after me next with an offer, and when they do, I will make them a counter offer with my rifle." He chuffed through his nostrils and kept eating.

The sound of the helicopter outside grew louder for a few moments and then faded. Wolf was suddenly a little claustrophobic. He looked out the window, wanting to be outside, surveying the surroundings. He thought about Young's long, animalistic strides as he barreled down that trail.

Martin looked at him and nodded his head towards the wall. "Take my rifle. My cell phone is on the counter. You'll have to climb the rocks behind the house for reception. I'll be there when I'm done."

From the rock outcropping behind the house, Wolf could see three hundred and sixty degrees. To the southwest were the two tall peaks. In between him and the peaks were a few lower rocky hills and the miles of dense forest that he'd just traveled through.

On the other side of the peaks were the 2Shoe Ranch and a jet-black sky that flickered with lightning within. The helicopter was gone, probably grounded because of the storm.

To the west was the highway. Wolf could see a few silent cars in the distance weaving their way north into Cave Creek Canyon.

Wolf squinted and studied the expanse of forest below. He couldn't see any movement, but that didn't mean no one was there.

He swiveled north and gazed at the countless layers of blue mountains in between him and the furthest point he could see, which was probably a mountain in Wyoming. The highway strung its way through the low valleys into the distance, straight past the Clover Mine—Connell-Brack Mining Corp's flagship gold mine opened over fifty years ago by Wallace Connell, Gary's father—one of six they owned in the western United States.

Streams of dust rose from the trees, which must have been mining trucks driving the maze of dirt roads inside the forest. Tailings piles poked up into view every now and again. The sprawl of activity was immense.

Wolf knew that Clover Mine's operations were strictly underground—not surface mined with an open pit like the Cresson Mine he'd seen outside of Cripple Creek to the south.

From here, the old run-down house that Martin and Dennis had now both mentioned was out of sight, just on the other side of the slope to the north. One thing was for sure, though—there was a heck of a lot of distance between the mining operations and where the old house was. If the Clover Mine had extended that far, it covered at least two miles underground.

Wolf sat down facing south, keeping some rocks between him and the forest below just in case Young was taking aim at that very second. He took out the cell phone and called Rachette.

"Hello?" The voice sounded very faint, but Wolf could hear the urgency in Rachette's voice just the same.

"Hey. It's me."

Silence. "Hi, Mom. Look, I'm kind of busy right now." A pause. "What? Hold on just a second."

Wolf could hear his ragged breathing and footsteps crunching in his earpiece.

"What's going on? You all right?" Rachette mumbled.

"Yeah. I'm fine. Just let me know where you guys are."

"I don't know." His voice was louder than it needed to be. "Fine, Mom. Fine." Another pause, then his voice lowered. "I'm with Vickers, we found your motorcycle, and we found an ATV."

"It's Young's. He's after me."

Rachette sounded like he was trying not to move his lips. "Where are you right now?"

"I'd rather not say, just in case. Where are you guys going?"

"Uh-huh. Yes." There was a full ten seconds of rustling and wind rushing into the phone. "Sorry. We're basically going to set up a perimeter around Gary's ranch. They think you're coming after him. Gary came and gave us a big speech last night. Vickers is heading the search up, and he keeps telling everyone to shoot first. Talking about how dangerous you are."

Wolf nodded, thinking.

Rachette's voice was loud. "All right, Mom! Easy!" Another pause. "Hey."

"Yeah."

"You didn't kill Connell, did you?" Rachette's voice was almost inaudible.

"No. It was Young. And Gary. They set me up."

"It was your knife found at the scene of Mark Wilson's stabbing," came out of Rachette's mouth in a whispered tumble. "All right! Bye, Mom. I love you too. I have to go. Okay. I know. Bye."

Wolf stared at the phone, then glared into the forest below. "Damn." He pecked out a text message on the ancient phone.

"You get bad reception?" Martin was standing behind him.

"No, it was fine. Just ... other problems." He held up the phone to Martin, who took it and pushed a few buttons, then eyed the screen. "Construction site? What's so important about the construction site?"

Wolf turned to the north. "Can you take me to the Silversmith property?"

"Sure. Now?"

"Now. And we'll need rifles."

CHAPTER 33

RACHETTE POCKETED the phone and looked at the ominous clouds to the south. The dark-green curtain of rain flickered within, and then a finger of lightning lunged out of the clouds, striking just at the base of the mountain, followed a few seconds later by a deafening crack of thunder.

If there was one thing Rachette didn't like, it was lightning. If he'd had his way, they'd have been off this exposed peak the second the helicopter was grounded, which was a good fifteen minutes ago.

Apparently Vickers had finally got the hint, or felt one of his few un-gelled hairs lift, because he was barking through the radio for everyone to get down the mountain and seek shelter.

Those people who were on the east end of the mountain went east, those on the west, west. Rachette was in between. Vickers was west, so he turned and jogged east.

"Rachette." The radio crackled.

Rachette rolled his eyes and turned with his hands up. "Yeah!"

Vickers craned his finger.

Rachette ran to Vickers, who waved him past with a whirling hand.

"Give me the phone." Vickers voice bounced behind Rachette.

"What?"

"You heard me. Give it now."

Rachette cursed himself, dug in his pocket and pitched the phone back.

The sky flashed bright and the air shook with ear-splitting thunder.

"Jesus! Jeez." Rachette corrected himself in the face of imminent death. "We've gotta get down, Sarge."

Vickers caught the phone and slowed to a stop, looking at the screen.

Rachette turned and walked back up the trail to him. "Sir, we've gotta get down, now."

Vickers took out his own phone and pressed a number. "Sergeant Vickers here. I need someone to triangulate the following cell phone number as soon as possible." He paused. "Because Wolf just called from that number."

He relayed the number, hung up, and flung the phone at Rachette as he ran past and down the trail.

Rachette caught the phone as a cold drop of rain smacked him on the cheek. The screen was illuminated with an incoming message scrawled across it. He furrowed his brow and looked down the trail. Vickers was out of sight.

Another bolt of lightning struck close with a boom of thunder.

Rachette winced as he unlocked the phone, erased the message, pocketed it, and ran as fast as he could.

CHAPTER 34

WOLF AND MARTIN came out of the trees into a bare, flat patch of forest where the old house stood. It faced north, and the view was immense. The mining operations were in the distance, and beyond that the unending waves of mountains.

The siding of the house had long been stripped its paint, leaving the boards a bleached ash color. Every board in the structure was warped, ejecting most of the nails, causing the entire house to lean slightly downhill; and every window was punched out with just a few hanging shards of glass remaining or none at all.

The air smelled like old bones, and the continuous buzz of insects was deafening.

Wolf slapped a hand on a hot board on the back of the house, half expecting the structure to tip forward. He walked the perimeter to a vacant window and peeked inside.

The floors were gray, with warped boards covered with dirt, rocks and twigs. A workbench stood against one wall with two vises affixed. Underneath it was a wad of sticks and grasses, like a family of raccoons had built a den. A kitchen counter drooped off the wall, looking like it would fall at the same time the house tipped forward. There was no sink in the counter, and no furniture anywhere.

"When did they leave?"

"They left in 1996." Martin's voice was muffled on the other side of the house.

The year Dad died.

Wolf walked around to the front, wiping a spider web strand off his face.

The sun went behind the clouds and a low distant rumble shook the air.

Wolf stopped, remembering his conversation with Dennis. "Bill Chester."

Martin came around the house and met him in front. "What?"

"That's the guy who bought the house. Do you know who that is? Bill Chester."

Martin shook his head.

Wolf looked up at the dark clouds, seeing a thin strand of lightning over the hill they'd just come down. "I don't get it. How do you know they sold it? Were you friends with the Silversmith? Did you talk to him about the sale?"

Martin tilted up his hat. "I was friends with him and his wife. They had a daughter, about ten years old. One day I came down here and they were gone." He snapped his fingers. "Just like that. I remember the day. There had been a big storm the night before, and I wanted to see how they were, to talk about it with someone. It was a lot of rain and wind." He shrugged. "I came here, and they were just gone."

Wolf nodded. "And? How did you find out they had sold the place?"

"A week later I asked one of my sources in town about it. She said they had sold the place for a lot of money to a man.

Over one million dollars." He glanced at Wolf, and gave a nod of his head, as if that had cleared everything up.

"Keep going. You said they sold it to the mine. Like I said, I heard it was a guy named Bill Chester who bought it."

Martin narrowed his eyes and held up a finger. "I watched this property for months. There was never a soul who set foot on this property. Not a single person who claimed their prize. I often hunt these woods, just like I did back then. I go all the way to the boundary of the mine. And back then I would make it a point to come here every time, to see if there was something new. One day, I walked from below, up to the house, and that was the first time I heard an angry rumble underneath the ground. And then I knew. They had sold the property to the mine.

"Over the years, they've hollowed out the ground underneath our feet. I'm sure of it. Look over there." He pointed to the east. "See where there is a clearing in the forest? That's a hole. The forest fell straight into the ground where they were digging underneath."

Wolf saw the spot. The ground wasn't visible, but there was an area of missing trees.

A warm spray of liquid hit Wolf on the right side of his face. He brought his hand up with a flinch, just as he saw Martin crumple forward in a twisting motion. An instant later he heard the rolling boom of a high-powered rifle.

Wolf lunged forward and caught Martin before he hit the ground and pulled him back. Just then the air sounded like it had been ripped, and the ground exploded into a spray of dust. A bullet ricocheted into the distance with a loud whine, and then there was another rifle report.

Wolf turned with Martin under his arm and stumbled to the front of the house and around the corner, to the opposite side of where the shots were coming from.

He set Martin down and looked at his wound. A ragged-looking exit wound bled profusely from underneath the collarbone, and there was a neat entry-wound at the top of his shoulder. Wolf took off his backpack, pulled out a shirt and began applying pressure to the bleeding hole.

"Martin. Can you hear me?"

Martin didn't respond.

Wolf checked his pulse. It seemed weak.

The boards exploded above him as four consecutive shots rang out.

No doubt it was Young.

Martin was bleeding but Wolf had seen worse in the field, and seen those soldiers survive in the end. Judging from the amount of blood, it looked like the bullet had missed arteries, but being so close to the heart there was no telling what damage had been done.

He dug in Martin's pocket and took out his cell phone. There was no reception.

Another three shots tore through the boards, and a blast of stinging splinters hit Wolf in the back of his head and neck. He winced and lay down flat.

Again, the image of Young, running on the trail at full speed with a calm face, flashed through Wolf's mind.

CHAPTER 35

YOUNG STOOD MOTIONLESS, staring through the scope.

He was getting impatient, so he fired another three rounds into the house, trying to miss high.

His ears rang, and the smell of gunpowder filled his nose. He flexed his shoulder against the butt of the rifle and smiled. He felt alive.

He couldn't help himself with the old man. It was just too perfect an opportunity to pass up—a perfect way to instill a little fear into Wolf, to get everyone's juices pumping.

He estimated twelve to twenty minutes. That was when he'd be finished pulling the life out of David Wolf's body, and the old guy would be before or after. He didn't care. He couldn't tell whether his first shot had hit high or just right. Either way, the old guy wasn't going to be moving far.

He glanced at his watch and added twenty minutes to the big hand, setting the deadline. It may well have been a prophecy carved in stone and given to him by the hand of God.

His body vibrated with anticipation.

And it would have to be close. Hand to hand.

The side of the house bounced in the scope as he stifled a laugh.

He'd always been an overachiever, putting unrealistic demands on himself, but they were demands he always met.

A few seconds later Wolf flew into view, sprinting full speed away from the house.

He popped one round behind him and watched.

Wolf ran straight away from the old house, straight for a ridgeline in the distance, and then he did the unexpected. Instead of going over it and out of sight, he turned left and started slogging up the side. He kept himself behind cover, sheltered behind the ridge most of the time, save for a glimpse of the top of his head every few feet.

Young pulled the rifle away and strapped it across his back, keeping a sharp eye on Wolf's pathetically slow movement up the side of the hill.

He looked at the hypotenuse leg he'd have to cover to beat Wolf to his destination, then back to Wolf, who was resolute in his dumb tactic.

Wolf was the first kill. The old guy would be second.

Young sucked a breath in and took off at full speed.

CHAPTER 36

Wolf's lungs sucked hard for air as he trundled up the slope. His vision tunneled as his brain groped for oxygen that just wasn't coming. His leg muscles were slow and unresponsive as he neared the top of the ridgeline, but he dug deep and somehow kept his pace steady.

Wolf knew that Young would have to cover at least double the distance Wolf had, with a steep incline of his own to negotiate. Wolf thought of Young on the trail again, and a shot of adrenaline coursed through his body.

As he reached the final ten feet of the slope, crawling on his hands and feet, muscles twitching involuntarily, he knew he probably wouldn't have a second to rest when he got to the top.

With agonizing strain on every fiber in his body, he reached the top, pulled his Glock, turned left in a squat and scanned for Young.

The ridge below was heavily treed, sloping down into a saddle, then back up to where the shots had come from. He wheezed loud as he scanned the woods from left to right.

Just then, a hard blow hit him on the back of the head,

toppling him forward. His face hit the ground first, ripping his lip down while pebbles scraped against his teeth. His Glock was wrenched from his hand, and then a huge hand gripped his shirt, lifted him up, yanked the rifle off his shoulder, and dropped him.

Then there was nothing.

Wolf huffed, coughing dirt, rocks, and needle fragments from his throat, then got on all fours and shook his head. His vision and thoughts cleared at the same time, and he jumped to his feet and turned around, ready to defend himself.

Young sat on a rock ten feet away with an amused grin. He looked at his watch, a sporty diver's watch that looked like a dainty children's model on his enormous wrist. "Take your time. Catch your breath."

Wolf narrowed his eyes, still sucking air. He eyed Young and brushed debris from his face and arms.

Young breathed heavily also, but in a way that didn't contort his face at all. He was staring at Wolf, studying his every move. Next to him were two rifles propped against a rock with Wolf's pistol next to them.

Young had on a skintight black shirt that revealed every nook and cranny of his heavily muscled frame. Wolf estimated him at three hundred pounds of pure muscle, and as he'd proven on two occasions now, it was muscle that was strong enough to move itself with the agility of a cat.

There was zero-percent chance that Wolf could best the man in a hand-to-hand fight. He wasn't being pessimistic—it was just a fact that needed to be taken into account.

Wolf took off his backpack and threw it down on the ground, eyeing Young's waist. A SEAL knife housed in a black Kydex sheath was strapped to his belt on his right, and it didn't look like he had a pistol.

"Oh, you're looking at this thing?" Young took out the knife, extended his arm, and dropped it ceremoniously next to Wolf's pistol. Then he looked at his watch again.

"You late for an appointment?" Wolf moved his right leg a little, feeling the lump of steel in the right front pocket of his Carhartt pants.

Young smiled and shook his head. "Not yet. I still have a few minutes."

Wolf's entire body flinched backwards as Young stood up, revealing his full, disturbing height.

Young laughed. "You're the big man around here, huh? Big army ranger." He smiled, shook his head and widened his eyes. "I can't wait to get me some ranger pussy."

Wolf took a deep breath and whimpered.

A flash lit the darkened forest, followed immediately by deafening thunder, and Wolf cowered, squinting towards the rapidly approaching storm.

CHAPTER 37

YOUNG STOPPED and tilted his head.

His face dropped, and his body sank with a disappointment that felt like the blood had been sucked through his feet. Then a rage welled up that he knew he wouldn't be able to contain, and it made him even more livid. His teeth mashed together so hard that he almost cracked a molar.

This was the man Gary had said he needed to watch out for?

The sniveling wimp was acting like a little girl. This guy wasn't a former ranger, or if he had been, it'd screwed him up bad.

This guy was facing a fight to the death, one that would ultimately determine the honor in which one man would die. And he was worried about lightning? There was no way this man had what it took to become a ranger. He was a fraud.

Young took a step forward, watching the coward raise his hands and lower his eyes in a defeated posture. It was one of the most revolting things he had ever seen. At that moment he decided to let his rage go on this one.

"Give a dying man a final request?" The little pussy talked fast.

Young stopped. Just barely. "What's that?" he managed with a shaking voice.

"Let me have the knife?" He held out his hands and looked up with pleading eyes. "You know I don't have a chance without it."

Young stared at him for a few seconds. Then he smiled. Then he chuckled. Then his entire body flooded with endorphins as he shook with laughter until his eyes teared. Or maybe it was the cool rain that was steadily increasing. He opened his mouth to the sky and caught a few drops, then snapped his head down into a toothy grin, his eyes landing smack-dab on Wolf's.

"You almost had me going there." He pointed his finger. "I don't care how old, fat, and slow you are, that would be a dumb move on my part."

The cop's pathetic look didn't waver. In fact, it got worse, and his breathing increased, like he was having a panic attack or something.

Young turned around, picked up the knife, and flipped it to him on a low arc. The cop caught it with his left hand.

"Then again, I am that good." Young blanked his face. "And I very much want this to be interesting."

Young didn't kid himself. He knew the danger he'd just put himself in, giving a knife to a former ranger. He reached up and stroked the scar underneath his eye with a wide smile. But he'd been in his share of knife fights without a blade himself, with far more competent opponents. He tempered his confidence, knowing he'd probably just been baited. It would make the victory all the more satisfying.

Yeah. It was definitely interesting now.

Young smiled at the audacity of the man in front of him,

then checked his watch one last time. One minute left until his personal deadline. Plenty of time.

He crept forward in a low stance.

Wolf crouched as well, keeping the knife in his left hand.

A lefty? But his gun had been on his right hip. He'd have to be wary of a hand switch. Wolf held the blade forward, not even using a reverse grip. But that could change in the blink of an eye.

Wolf was baiting him again and again, keeping Young guessing.

Young stepped in fast, quickly getting slashed on the back of his wrist, missing a counter-attack as Wolf shuffled away, and then behind a tree.

He hopped back and sucked the blood mixed with rain, then bared his teeth. The adrenaline surged through his veins. Every muscle in his body screamed for the kill.

"Get some!"

Wolf came out on the offensive from behind the tree, faking high with a flurry of motion, then came in low with a sweeping upward strike. But Young was ready, bashing both his fists on the forearm with all the strength he could muster in such a short reaction, which was more than most bones on any man could handle.

Young connected, and as Wolf's forearm rebounded backwards, the knife tumbled out of his hand, flipped through the rain and bounced down the slope a good twenty feet; it slid out of sight, pushed by the deluge of rain.

"Ahh!" Wolf screamed like a woman and turned away, then fell to his stomach and writhed on the ground in pain.

"Get up!" A surge of disgust swept through Young again. The pussy hadn't lasted three seconds before giving up. Young stood over Wolf, who was on his knees with his ass in the air, turning his head, looking for Young over both shoulders.

Young gritted his teeth and thumped his hands on Wolf's back with unmerciful force. He dug his fingers into the skin as he wrenched Wolf sideways, then rolled him to face the most horrific death that no man could imagine in their worst nightmares.

Wolf turned onto his back and straightened his legs, keeping his arms tucked into his sides.

Young collapsed his weight onto Wolf's upper body the second his back touched the rain-soaked earth, then straddled his chest, crunching Wolf's arms to his sides with his massive legs.

Rain dripped off Young's nose as he bent down close and howled like a savage demon in Wolf's face. Young popped his eyes wide, bared his teeth and stuck out his tongue. Slobber strung out, and he exhaled hard from his nostrils, letting mucus fly, just to add to the effect.

Wolf stared back with a defiant expression.

Young grabbed hold of his neck with his gigantic hand and watched the expression change to determination.

In the end, it was always an expression of alarm—a realization that death was imminent, and that they were not ready. Like they had just remembered they'd forgotten the most important homework assignment of their life, forgotten to put their pants on before the big presentation.

Young slowly strengthened his grip, savoring the moment.

Then something went very wrong.

Wolf jolted, his knees bucking hard into Young's ass. Then he jolted again. Then Wolf was thrashing in a flurry of movement underneath him.

Deep apprehension suddenly filled Young. There was no pain, none at all, but there was a numb, pulling sensation that sent a wave of nausea from his intestines upwards. His instincts were screaming for him to get up. *Now.*

He rolled off Wolf and stood fast, and then the agony attacked his brain like a swarm of angry bees.

He had no control over the high-pitched squeal that came out of his throat as he opened his twitching legs and felt underneath. He raised a hand and watched in horror as the rain washed warm crimson globs up his forearm.

The cop had stabbed him in the ass, and now warm blood was gushing down each leg inside his pants. Pain multiplied with each second. His stomach twisted in agony and seemed to drop inside of him. It was beyond a foreign feeling. It was ridiculous. It was not happening.

Then a blow pounded him underneath the jaw with a violence he'd never felt before, and all went black.

CHAPTER 38

WOLF TWISTED the blade deep under Young's jaw, watching the big man's eyes un-focus as he collapsed straight forward into a lifeless heap. Keeping a close eye on Young's back for signs of movement, Wolf rolled the Leatherman multi-tool in his fingers, allowing the cool rain to wash off the blood and excrement.

He scrubbed his hands in mud, then wiped them on his pants, which were now soaked to the skin from the deluge of rain.

Folding the knife blade back into its housing, Wolf stopped short of kissing the Leatherman, deciding it would need a good boiling before he showed his trusty multi-tool the love it deserved, and shoved it back into his front pocket.

He quickly patted down Young, finding a cell phone in his pants pocket. He took the phone and continued his search.

Lightning struck nearby, followed immediately by a clap of thunder, and then the rain intensified even more. Wolf stood still, staring at Young's cargo pocket he'd just squeezed.

He reached inside and pulled out his father's ring.

Another lightning bolt jolted him out of his daze. He put the ring on, gathered his backpack and Glock, then got underneath an overhang in the rocks. He wiped his face and looked at the ring again, then he dug into the pack and pulled out Martin's cell phone. There were two bars of reception.

He dialed the station. Tammy Granger answered the call after one ring, and Wolf gave a detailed description of Martin's wounds and whereabouts, shouting over the sound of the rain.

"Wolf? Is that you?" the tinny voice screamed into the phone.

Wolf hung up.

Rain came in sheets, spraying him with a fine mist, and his wet tee shirt was sucking the heat from his body fast. He took it off and put on his jacket, which had remained relatively dry in the pack.

The rain was coming in at an angle from the southwest. He hoped Martin was keeping dry on the north side of the old house he'd just left him at.

Wolf stared at Young's hulking body slumped in the mud, looking like a dead rhinoceros.

If Young had been acting alone, then why had he been busy the last couple of days implicating Wolf as much as trying to eliminate him? Why plant Wolf's knife at the stabbing of Mark Wilson? Why frame Wolf for Connell's murder? Gary had to be behind it all.

Wolf stared into the rain and thought about all that had happened, and the motivations of everyone involved.

The answer was beginning to come into focus, and, if Wolf was right, it meant the past sixteen years of his life would have to be completely rethought.

After a few minutes, the rain let up to a drizzle and the sun burned bright through the clouds in the west.

He stood and loosened his painfully tight muscles and heard the faint whir of sirens. The highway below was hidden behind the receding white veil of rain, but the sirens were down there and getting closer. To the south, the air thumped as the helicopter took back to the skies and neared.

Wolf took out Martin's and Young's cellphones, and tossed Martin's far down the slope he'd climbed up earlier.

He thought about the text he'd sent to Rachette, and hoped he'd gotten his point across. Then he held up Young's cell phone to check the reception and battery, and knew there was one more message he needed to send. But he needed to get closer to that construction site first.

Wolf turned and squinted into the steamy woods below, then took off down the slope as fast as his sore muscles could take him.

CHAPTER 39

GARY LOOKED at his phone and swiveled to squint at the blazing sunset over the western valley from in front of the Connell estate's equipment shed.

It was from Young.

He stared at the screen and responded to the text message, then shoved the phone in his jeans pocket and closed his eyes to the warm light. His chest rose as he inhaled the sweet scent of wet sage; then it fell as he exhaled sixteen years of pent-up tension.

But it wasn't over. Not yet. He wasn't lighting another Behike yet.

Gary turned to Buck and Earl, who both leaned against the flatbed tow truck. Buck wiped a dollop of dark spit from his chin and went back to his stoic stillness.

"I just got word from Young. It's done." Gary thought Earl may have raised an eyebrow. "He's on his way here. We'll set everything up, and keep the cops preoccupied well into the morning hours. In the meantime, get over there and finish it now."

Buck's eyes narrowed and he pushed up the bill of his mesh trucker hat. "What if someone sees us workin'?"

Gary waved his hand. "So what? Nobody knows who you are. They'll think you're the night crew. In fact, if anyone asks, that's exactly what you are. But who's gonna ask? The cops? They'll be busy scraping Wolf's corpse out of the forest over here. They'll have plenty of other shit to worry about than checking into the legitimacy of a construction crew. Now get the hell out of here."

Earl and Buck moved fast for the doors of the hulking flatbed.

"Remember." They stopped and listened. "I want that ring."

They said nothing and got in.

Gary watched the diesel gurgle to life and speed away through the red mud. He needed his rifle, and he had some time to kill as he waited for Young and the corpse of the man he'd tried to help, but who just wouldn't listen.

Another wave of guilt lapped his mind. A scotch and cigar would help.

Gary almost barreled square into his father as he entered the trophy room.

"What are you doing up?"

The old fart stared at him with that look of disappointment he'd grown so accustomed to seeing his whole life.

"What? What is it this time, Dad? What are you upset about now?" Gary put a hand to his ear and leaned close.

His father's glare was ice. "What's going on?"

They stared at each other in silence. Gary wanted to tell him the good news, but, then again, he didn't like the assumption in his dad's look or his tone. It was all too familiar.

His dad never thought he could do it. It never mattered

what *it* was. It was always the same story. He was always guilty until proven innocent. Weak until proven strong. Gary was finished proving anything.

His dad's face curled in a humorless smile, thick with disgust. "You've done it, haven't you?"

"I've done what, Dad?"

"Well, son ..." He used the condescending tone Gary had grown to love. "You've single-handedly ruined us."

Gary stared at him coolly.

His father glared. His chin quivered harder as he wheezed. Then he shook his head, this time on purpose.

"Stephanie!" Gary yelled.

Silence echoed in the vast house.

His father's eyes widened. "And what will be left when all is said and done?" His father's face went still for the first time in years. "Nothing."

Gary controlled his breathing as he watched his father's lips rise to a snarl.

"Nothing will be left. There's not going to be a legacy, or anyone to leave it to. Not even your son. Oh," he laughed in Gary's face, "wait, that wasn't even your son. You're a goddam disapp—"

Gary reached his hand out and clutched his father's throat.

His father gurgled, and his hands came up, groping feebly at Gary's grip.

Gary squinted and looked out at the fleeting blaze of orange in the western windows. He struggled to keep his hand clenched on his father's warm, wrinkly neck as it collapsed under his fingers, so he let go, turned him around and grabbed him in a full-strength headlock. Then he picked up the walker in his other hand, and moved down the hall.

He slowed a little at the next window pane and squinted, put down the walker for a second, cleared a smudge with the side of his palm, then continued onward, with the gentle scrape of slippered feet trailing behind.

The kicking had stopped by the time he reached the end of the long hall. He opened a bedroom, hauled back and threw in his motionless father like a sack of leaves, chucked in the walker for good measure, and closed the door.

CHAPTER 40

RACHETTE SHOVED his hands deep in his jacket and looked at the bullet exit holes on the north side of the old house. It was easy enough to see where the shots had come from by squinting and looking through the hole towards the mountainside. Up near that very spot, two deputies were waving flashlight beams in the dusk.

Vickers looked into the woods towards the fading orange sunset.

"So?" Rachette stood next to Vickers.

"So what?"

"I talked to Tammy," Rachette said. "She says it was definitely Wolf who called in the location of the old man."

Vickers nodded, eyes unblinking.

"Why would Wolf do that? I'm telling you, it was this guy Young. That was his ATV way back there on the mountain behind Connell's ranch, and it was Young who shot this old guy." Rachette pointed up the hill towards the beams of light on the hillside. "From up there. Then Wolf probably dragged the old man out of danger." He pointed to the side of the house. "And Young blasted away at them."

Looking at the ground revealed nothing, however. It was a blank canvas, wiped clean of any evidence during the earlier deluge of rain.

Vickers pointed to the deputies up on the hill. "Thanks to your little phone call with Wolf, the triangulation pointed in that direction. At the old man's house. Wolf could have barged in on the old man, and maybe the old man fled. Maybe the old man ran here to get away from him, and Wolf picked him off from up there."

Rachette snorted. "Yeah, then the old man found a shirt on the ground here to press against the wound before he went into a coma. Come on. It was a third person who shot him. It was Young. And Wolf helped the guy and called it in."

Vickers got on the radio. "Wilson, what do you guys have up there?"

The radio scratched. "Nothing yet, sir."

Vickers studied the hillside, then the bullet holes again. "You've gotta go higher. Let me know the second you guys find anything. Where the hell are the K-9 units?"

A few seconds passed and then the radio hissed again. "They are on their way, sir. Within the hour," said a voice Rachette didn't recognize.

Vickers turned and walked away.

A state trooper van showed up twenty minutes later, full of boxed food and refreshments.

Night had fully set in and only the faintest light was still visible over the western peaks. Two vehicles' halogen lights shone a bright swath over the area. The men who weren't stuck on the side of the hill ate and laughed heartily, seeming to enjoy the adventure of the situation.

"The way Wolf hit that tree with his motorcycle, holy shit! I couldn't believe he got up, huh, Rachette?" Baine's voice was loud as he sat cross-legged among the other uniformed men, barking out his story to anyone who would listen.

Rachette turned his back and walked into the darkness. He took the final bite of his turkey sandwich, sucked down the last of his bottle of water, and watched Vickers.

Vickers was sitting near the edge of the lit area, staring at the ground, like he'd been doing for the past fifteen minutes.

Young existed. Rachette was sure of it now. He knew Vickers was wrestling with the same thoughts.

Suddenly Vickers jolted to attention and pulled his cell phone out of his pocket. Walking into the darkness, he put the cell to his ear.

Rachette stepped nearer, trying to hear the conversation.

Vickers nodded and pocketed the phone, and then he walked toward a deputy who sat smoking on the hood of an SUV, barked an order, and held out his hand.

The deputy fished in his pocket, produced some keys, and handed them over. Vickers opened the door and the deputy slid off the hood and walked away.

"Sergeant Vickers!" Rachette yelled.

Vickers propped a leg inside the truck and turned.

"Where you going?"

Vickers shook his head. "I've got some business to attend to. You've got your orders, deputy." He got in, fired up the engine, and drove away down the dirt road.

Rachette looked to the deputy who'd just given up his vehicle. "Where did he say he was going?"

The guy squinted and blew out a drag. "Didn't. Just said to get going once the K-9s get here. Said it would be any minute." He shrugged.

Rachette stared at the brake lights as they disappeared into the trees below, then sprinted over to Baine.

CHAPTER 41

WOLF COULD HEAR the chaos from over a half-mile away, but now that he was much closer, right against the security fence of the construction site, the diesel engine of the excavator and the boom of rock against steel that echoed up and down Cave Creek Canyon was deafening.

He was squatting next to a boulder against the north perimeter fence, opposite where he'd parked with Rachette the morning before.

There weren't any bright halogen lights glowing from within, like one would expect from a legitimate night-time construction operation. But his eyes had fully adjusted to the night, and he could see clearly enough.

He zipped up his coat and yanked his black winter hat down. It was cold, at least ten degrees colder at the bottom of the canyon, and just ten feet above the rushing river.

Wolf ducked behind the boulder and pulled out the binoculars from his backpack, then peeked over and pressed the frigid eyepieces to his face.

Thirty feet to the rear of the excavator stood a man carrying a rifle and a flashlight pointed at the mountain.

Wolf scanned the rest of the area, finding no one. It was a two-man show, and he recognized the silhouette behind the excavator as one of Gary's two ranch hands. He assumed the other was driving the rig.

He ducked behind the boulder again and pulled out Young's phone. There were no messages. Gary would still be at the ranch, waiting patiently for Young to show up with Wolf's dead body. But the clock was ticking. Gary was an impatient man, and smart. Sooner or later he would find out that Young was not coming, and when he did, Wolf wanted to be done here.

Wolf pocketed the phone, then shuffled out and brought the binoculars back to the excavator.

The machine's engine dropped to an idle, then shut off, plunging the night into relative silence.

The excavator sat still, bucket on the ground. A figure jumped down from the operator cab and walked towards the side of the mountain.

The rush of the river muted an animated conversation between the two men, but Wolf got the gist of it. The rear man pointed his light and walked fast toward the mountainside while the other followed closely behind. They had uncovered what they came to uncover.

Wolf looked up at the fence. It was topped with a spiral of razor wire, extending straight ahead to the river, then strung along the river to the other end of the construction site, where the gate stood wide open—a good hundred yards away.

The silhouettes of the two men seemed to disappear straight into the mountain.

Wolf wasted no time, sprinting along the fence to the edge and dropping to his belly to take a look. It was ten feet of steep incline, then a row of rocks along the river. He swiveled and slid feet first, then hopped along the boulders in a fast jog.

At the end of the fence line, Wolf crawled to the top of the slope and peeked over.

A haphazard group of rock piles surrounded the steaming excavator. The site looked like a bomb had gone off somewhere high above, sending down tons of rubble.

Wolf realized it was the scree field the construction crew had been busy removing earlier, completely shoveled away from the side of the mountain and now strewn about on the ground. Where it used to be, now yawned a tall cave, flickering yellow from the light within.

Wolf sprinted through the gate, his steps crunching louder to his own ears as he moved further from the river. The cave bobbled in his vision as he stepped fast, finally reaching a pile of rubble just as a beam pointed out of the hole. He crouched, pulled his Glock, and looked over the rocks.

One of the men jangled a set of keys in his hand and jogged by.

Wolf ducked down, just barely keeping undetected.

A few seconds later, a diesel engine, this time a truck outside the fence-line, fired up, and then tires munched nearer.

Wolf stayed down as headlights streamed shadows across the gouged mountain. The lights turned away towards the river, then the truck backed into position with a beep that echoed through the canyon.

The engine went silent, a door slammed shut, and the keys jangled as the man stepped back towards the cave.

Wolf scurried to the edge of the rock pile and looked.

A black flatbed tow truck shone in the moonlight, looking brand new. Probably the best money could buy. Probably bought just for the occasion.

A series of metallic clacks pierced the air, then a motor whirred as the tilt tray slid back, angling until the rear scraped against the ground. Then there was a high-pitched whine and a gleaming cable with a thick metal hook on the end bobbled down the ramp.

After a few seconds, one of them, Buck, or Earl, stopped the winch and pulled the cable out of sight into the cave.

Wolf walked silently around the pile, then straight to the opening.

"Stop what you're doing and put your hands up." He trained the Glock on the guy without the cable.

The two men turned with wide eyes and put their arms up, which sent the beams of their flashlights pointing up to the ceiling.

The sudden change in lighting gave all three of them the same idea at once, and when the two men shot lightning-quick glances at each other, Wolf dove forward.

Wolf was only halfway to the nearest man when they both turned off their flashlights, sending the cave into pitch-black. Wolf groped through empty air, brushing up against the back of one of the men's cowboy hats.

He clamped his left arm around the guy's head and sat down to bring him to the ground. The man buckled, and when Wolf felt his butt hit the floor, he yanked the man backwards so that they both lay flat, with the man on top of him acting as a shield.

A few feet away, the cave lit up with a massive cone of flame from the other man's pistol.

Wolf shot four times in a tight circle around where the blast had been, then slammed the butt of his Glock into the head of the man he held, hoping he'd connected with the temple.

The man on top of Wolf struggled with a strength he wasn't expecting, kicking and bucking back, his shoulders digging into Wolf's chest. Before Wolf could react, a slicing pain seared through his right thigh.

Wolf went berserk, rolling the man to the left and clubbing him in the head with repeated blows until he went limp.

Wolf pulled his arm out from under the man and blinked fast. His vision swam with fuzzy circles, and a tone whined in his ears. He slid his hand along the ground, and his finger glanced off a hard metal cylinder. It was the flashlight.

He picked it up with his left hand and extended his arm up to the side.

He pointed the dark flashlight carefully, then pointed the gun. He took a deep breath and clicked the flashlight on.

A thunderous bang flashed to his front and right as the air above his left wrist rippled painfully against his skin.

He aimed the beam and fired twice into the other man's head.

·

CHAPTER 42

BUCK SAT DEAD, two holes in his head, still holding the .45 revolver in a loose grip against the dirt.

It was Buck. He was the one with the thick gray mustache, Wolf remembered.

Wolf swung the flashlight beam through the thick smoke towards Earl, who lay on top of Wolf's leg, still unmoving and bleeding steadily above his eye. Wolf checked his pulse, which was strong.

The stench of gunpowder was thick in the closed space, stinging Wolf's eyes and obscuring the view within the cave.

He grunted, pulled his leg out from under Earl, and stood, his entire body shaking with adrenaline.

His black Carhartt pants were sliced on the right thigh. He unbuckled his belt and pulled them down for a look. The cut was a few inches long, but shallow and would clot soon.

Buck's flashlight had tumbled next to his feet, so Wolf picked it up and clicked it on too, then propped it against Buck's leg to point upward. He stripped the men of their weapons, tied Earl's hands behind his back with his belt and turned to the cave, finally registering what lay inside.

An old green Colorado license plate hung on one screw from a dirty rear bumper of a 1980s Chevy Suburban. The entire thing was so caked with dust that it was almost invisible against the surrounding brown rock walls and roof of the cavern.

Wolf swept his hand on the tailgate, revealing a cream-colored paint job below, then walked along the passenger side of the truck, stopping at the rear passenger window.

Despite the adrenaline pumping through his veins, and despite half expecting it, his heart sped faster as he swept the dust off the rear window with his palm, revealing a dark-brown tuft of hair matted against the glass. It was unmistakably human.

He raked the forearm of his jacket across the window, bringing the entire head into view. Red fabric with a dark-green triangular pattern was visible below the hairline. Underneath the clothing was emaciated gray skin, sucked deep against adolescent-sized vertebrae. Wolf's heart ached as he swept the beam forward, revealing a black-haired doll lying face down on the bone-thin pair of gray legs.

Wolf took a deep breath and moved to the front passenger window. He rubbed his sleeve again and peered in. Shining the flashlight beam inside the car revealed the wide-open mouth of what he could only assume was the Silversmith's dead wife. Her lips were shriveled, her gums gone, making the teeth look unnaturally large. The bottom jaw hung too low for the living, and her shoulder-length hair was a wispy gray mess that looked very brittle. Around her neck hung a necklace of blue turquoise circles set in silver disks.

Wolf pushed his thumb on the door handle and pulled. The door clunked and swung open, and a thin avalanche of dirt cascaded from the roof.

He let the cloud settle, then shone the beam inside, revealing the dead body of the Silversmith in the driver's seat. He wore a denim jacket with turquoise beaded tassels on his breast pockets. Black hair spiked out underneath a gray cowboy hat, reminding Wolf of Martin's hat of similar design. The man's lips sagged low, revealing the front bottom teeth, and his eyelids were sunk deep into his sockets.

Wolf pointed the light back to the woman. He took a deep breath, blocking out the faint beef-jerky smell, and leaned in. He reached down with his thumb and forefinger and lifted the dead woman's left wrist. With the sound of tiny twigs breaking, the arm rose, almost weightless in Wolf's grip. He twisted the back of the hand clockwise, revealing all of the fingers.

A silver ring, inlaid with a bright red-orange coral stripe, identical to the one on Wolf's pinkie finger now, gleamed in the light.

CHAPTER 43

WOLF STEPPED out of the cave, sucked in the cool fishy air of the river, and bent over and coughed, clearing the stale oxygen from his lungs. Just then a pair of headlights came into view through the construction-site gates.

He stood tall and squinted, seeing the dark, unmistakable shape of turret lights on a Ford Explorer.

A flashlight clicked on a few yards away, and a beam lanced Wolf's vision. "There's your cavalry," said a loud voice behind the light. It was Gary.

Wolf grabbed his holstered Glock.

"Drop it. Now," Gary said.

Wolf paused a beat and tossed the Glock a few feet to the side, knowing Gary would have a gun trained on him, held by a steady hand with true aim.

The SUV rocked to a stop in the parking lot and the door opened with a squeak. The two peaks and a circle of the SCSD logo were painted on the side.

"Hi Gary," Wolf said, watching Vickers step out of the SUV.

Gary lowered the flashlight and approached Wolf.

"Over here!" Gary yelled, waving the beam towards Vickers.

Vickers stood next to the vehicle, peering through the gates for a few moments, and then walked towards them.

"Your good man on the inside. Sergeant Vickers," Wolf said.

Gary stepped near, revealing a black leather-gloved hand pointing a .45 revolver with a long barrel, much like the one Buck had had inside the cave. Gary's expressionless, cleanly shaven mouth was the only visible part of his face underneath his leather hat.

He moved closer and pushed up the brim, revealing his ice-blue eyes in the moonlight. He walked to the Glock and pulled it back with his boot. Then he tucked the flashlight under his arm and bent to pick it up, all the while keeping the barrel of his revolver locked on Wolf's chest.

"What's going on?" Vickers was twenty yards away, approaching cautiously with his own pistol drawn.

"Look what I found." Gary holstered his revolver and beckoned Vickers with Wolf's Glock.

Vickers was wide-eyed, aiming his own gun at the ground in front of Wolf's feet, walking slow and deliberate. He flicked an imploring look towards Gary.

Gary ignored Vickers, aimed the Glock at Wolf, and stepped backwards to his original position, putting them in a triangle formation.

"Gary, don't shoot." Vickers held up a hand. "Don't do anything you'll regret. We'll take him in and do this right. I know you're upset about Derek, but we've gotta do this right, sir."

Wolf narrowed his eyes and looked at Vickers. The dynamic between the two was different than he expected. "Vickers," Wolf said, "listen to me. Point your gun at Gary."

Vickers looked at Wolf and then did a double take of the

cave entrance. He looked over his shoulder as if noticing the piles of rubble for the first time. Then he glared at Gary and put his other hand underneath the butt of his pistol.

"What the hell is going on?"

Wolf spread his fingers. "I've just figured out Gary's secret. That's what's going on."

"You see, Sergeant Vickers," Gary interjected in a loud voice, "sixteen years ago, a landslide covered this hole, along with a car." He pointed the flashlight to the cave entrance and lowered his voice. "In that car was a family."

Vickers furrowed his brow and looked towards the cave.

"Sergeant Wolf here just shot my men inside as they were trying to pull out the vehicle. That's why I called you, to let you know what we found. Then Wolf here showed up."

Wolf snorted. "Vickers. Listen. Sixteen years ago, Gary *buried* this vehicle with a family he murdered inside of it. He forced them to sell him their land, then killed them to keep it secret, and buried them here. I have proof. But you need to disarm Gary now, and I'll explain everything. Point your gun at him."

"Don't listen to him, son," Gary's voice boomed.

"Shut up! Both of you." Vickers looked pained as he volleyed glances between them.

"Sergeant Vickers." Gary's voice was barely audible over the rushing river.

Vickers lifted his gun and pointed it at Gary. "What the hell were your men doing uncovering this hole?"

"Sergeant Vickers, I'm going to ask you to do something, and then I want you to do it." Gary's voice was smooth and confident. "Please take a look inside that hole. You'll see that this man killed my two men in cold blood. It will all make sense soon, son. I promise you."

Vickers inhaled fast, looking at the cave entrance, then to Gary again.

Wolf turned his palms out. "Sergeant Vickers, don't listen to—"

"Shut up!" Vickers pointed his pistol at Wolf.

Wolf flinched as a loud explosion lit the night.

Vickers's head jerked back, and then with an involuntary muscle twitch his gun went off with a deafening blast of its own.

Wolf dropped flat to his belly as the air above his head hissed, a bullet passing just inches from his skull.

Vickers tipped backwards with both hands still clutching the smoking pistol. Then his knees buckled, and his lifeless body flopped sideways into an unnatural-looking contortion.

Gary's gun steamed in the moonlight. His eyes were wide and he was grinning. "Holy shit!" Gary bent at the hip and scanned Wolf with mock concern. "That was close! I should have just shot him when he walked up here."

Wolf shook his head and pushed up on his hands and knees. "What are you doing, Gary?"

Gary turned to Wolf. "What am I doing? The question is, what are you doing?" He glanced to the sky in mock thought. "Let's see. You shot the man who took your job as sheriff, stabbed your ex-wife's boyfriend, took out an old man in the woods, killed three of my men, and now you've put a bullet in the guy who was next in line for your job." He shook his head. "You've gone crazy."

Wolf's eyes narrowed. "I only killed two of your men, Gary. That's the first kink in your story that you'll want to get straight. Earl's unconscious in there, but he'll be fine. Or, I don't know, maybe you want to go in there and finish him off, just to get another kill under your belt." Wolf shook his head, looking over at Vickers. "You have quite a mess on your hands. What were Buck and Earl doing just now? Towing that Suburban with the dead family in it to one of your mines? Going to bury it a mile deep? How are you going to finish that job now? By yourself?"

Gary shrugged. "Exactly. That is, after I set it up to look like you killed Vickers." He kept the Glock aimed at Wolf, walked to Vickers, and pried the other department-issue Glock from his hand.

Gary faced Wolf and looked at the two nearly identical guns. He pointed the one in his right hand, raised an eyebrow, and then pulled it back. Then he pointed the one in his left, then lowered them both with a grin. The grin vanished as he dropped the right pistol on the ground, sending it skidding to a halt at least five yards from Wolf, and then stepped towards Wolf.

Wolf caught a flicker of movement in his peripheral vision behind Gary.

Gary stepped close. "You're still wearing that goddamn ring. If you would have just left that ring alone," he sighed, "you wouldn't be taking your last breaths right now."

Wolf snorted. "It's not my fault you're a low-life murderer."

Gary sneered and raised the pistol.

"Did you kill my father, Gary? Tell me that. You owe me that much." Wolf glared. "Or were you a coward, hiring out that piece of dirty work? Or maybe your dad did it for you?"

Gary hesitated and lowered the gun. His eyebrows peaked for an instant, and then his gaze steeled. "I'm so sorry, son. I'm sorry it didn't work out." He raised the gun again.

"So you did," Wolf said. "I can't believe it."

Gary's hand shook and he lowered the gun a few degrees. "Your father knew too much about this, and now you do, too. I'm sorry." Gary aimed straight at Wolf's chest.

"Hey! Hey! Hey!" A screaming voice came from the direction of the river.

Wolf dropped and rolled to his right as four pops echoed

through the canyon. Wolf finished his roll, scrambled forward, and dove for his Glock.

With as much concentration as he could muster, Wolf plucked it from the dirt and raised it up, but before he could aim, Gary landed next to him, his face bouncing off the ground. His eyes locked on Wolf's for a brief instant, and then the light within went out, and Gary was still.

Wolf braced Gary's arm and pried the gun out of his hand. "Took you long enough!" he yelled.

Rachette stepped away from the excavator into the moonlight. "You know me, my aim sucks. I had to get close."

CHAPTER 44

"ARE YOU KIDDING ME?" Rachette stared at Wolf, pointing his yolk-covered fork at the cell phone pressed against his ear. "Okay. Yeah, I'm with him now." Rachette rolled his eyes. "I don't know. You guys have it covered? Okay, talk to you soon."

Wolf raised an eyebrow and shoveled another bite of eggs and hash browns into his mouth. Then he surveyed the dining room of the Sunnyside Café, looking for the new girl again to get a third order of eggs and bacon started.

Rachette slapped the phone on the table, sipped his coffee, and sat back. "They found Gary's father dead this morning."

The new girl came to the table. "You guys doing okay?"

Rachette squinted, raised his eyebrows, and leaned forward without a smile. "I'm doing just fine," he said in a throaty voice.

"Okay." She nodded and stared blankly at Rachette for a beat. Then she shook her head and turned to Wolf with a smile. "And how about you?"

"I'll take another order of bacon and eggs, thanks."

"Jeez, that's quite an appetite you have there." She topped off their coffees.

He finished the rest of his plate in two bites and scooted it toward her.

"Another order coming right up." She sang the words and swayed her slender hips towards the kitchen.

Rachette turned his head and watched her go, then turned to Wolf with raised eyebrows. "She is into you."

Wolf stared at Rachette expectantly.

Rachette leaned forward on his elbows. "Oh, yeah. So that was Baine. They found Gary's father this morning."

"And?"

"Apparently he was heaped on the floor with a broken neck, his walker upside down next to him. Strangled. Gary's fingerprints on his neck."

Wolf shook his head and gazed out the window.

The sun flashed and dimmed behind low clouds skating across the sky above town. The window next to the booth shook with a low rumble, and outside pines bowed back and forth with bouncing limbs. A fierce wind of a fall cold front was tormenting the valley, and Wolf hoped it was decent enough weather for his brother's funeral tomorrow, though it wasn't looking good. Given the nature of the occasion, he guessed it really didn't matter. It would be a shitty day any way you cut it.

Wolf thumbed the empty spot on his pinkie finger and stared out the window.

Rachette cleared his throat. "The Connells killed your father, didn't they?"

Wolf nodded slowly. "For sixteen years I thought that ring I was wearing was a connection to my Navajo heritage, not a dead man's matching wedding band." He stared at the swaying trees. "The Connells must have freaked out the first time they saw me wearing it."

"I've never heard the official story," Rachette said. "How did your father die all those years ago?"

"It was unsolved. A shooting with no evidence to go on. Just a traffic stop that went horribly wrong. There were no official suspects. No knowledge of the vehicle he pulled over. Nothing. Two .22s were lodged in his head, no bullet casings found at the scene, and that's it.

"He was shot the day after the Connells buried the car in Cave Creek Canyon. He must have been investigating that slide ... maybe even found the ring there. Or who knows. The point is, he got too close. And the Connells killed him to keep their secret safe."

"What about Burton? You think he was in on it the whole time? And that's how he became sheriff all those years ago? By having a hand in your dad's death?"

Wolf shook his head. "I don't think he's that type of man. I've seen him do too many good things in my day." He took another sip of coffee. "But I'll be checking."

Rachette squirmed, propped his elbows on the table, and buried his face in his hands.

"What?"

"You have no clue how close I was to not coming down to the construction site. I had no idea what was going on. I was beginning to think that Young didn't exist. I really thought you'd gone off the deep end for a while there." He stared Wolf in the eye. "I'm sorry."

Wolf laughed and shook his head. "You're forgiven."

The waitress came with another plate and swiveled it in front of Wolf.

He sat up straight and thanked her with a smile, then watched her blush as she tucked her hair behind her ear and walked away.

"I told you," Rachette whispered.

Wolf dug into his plate. "Drink your coffee."

He inhaled half of the food, then set down his fork, now thinking he might have made a mistake ordering the third plate.

Rachette sat back. "So the Connells tried to buy the property from the Navajo family all those years ago. And?" He rolled his hand towards Wolf.

"Maybe they tried to buy it. Maybe they just walked into their house, put a gun to their heads and made them sign. Who knows?

"But they got the property and covered their bases, leaving a convoluted paper trail so no one would find out it was the mining company behind the purchase. And they made the price high enough that it would be believable that the family just up and disappeared. With over a million bucks, a lot of people would just up and leave to go start a new life."

Rachette narrowed his eyes. "Then they shoot the family, and bury them into the side of the mountain?"

Wolf stared into nothing, remembering his conversation with Martin. "There was a big storm with a lot of rain that day they disappeared. The Connells shot them, then put the family in one of those caves, then set a blast, making it look like the storm set off a big landslide. The landslide was a huge deal, I remember now. It was right around my dad's death. When he died, I had scoured the papers on the day of his death for any clues ... anything about the man who'd shot him. I remember that landslide being in the papers. But the news of it had taken a back seat to my father's death." Wolf stared out the window.

"Why wouldn't they put them in the mine? Get rid of the bodies there?" Rachette shook his head.

Wolf shrugged. "Not sure. There must have been some deterrent."

"So your father had to have known the truth about that slide, and the Connells killed him because of it."

Wolf nodded. "And that kept them in the clear for sixteen

years, until the Cave Creek Canyon highway-expansion project sprang up. They knew the bodies would be uncovered, and I would be right there pulling them out—right there seeing that identical ring to the one I would be wearing on my finger."

"And you'd put it all together soon after." Rachette scrunched his face. "But why didn't they just kill you? What was with that whole offering you a job thing?"

Wolf shook his head and thought about the pained look on Gary's face before Rachette shot him. "I think Gary really did think of me as the son he never had. And he probably felt guilt over killing my father or something. Probably trying to pay some karmic debt with me." Wolf shrugged. "I don't know. He let me stay on that ranch for years without me paying a cent.

"Offering me that job, he probably figured he could kill two birds with one stone—pay me massive amounts of money to feel better about himself, and get me out of the picture at the same time."

Rachette gazed out the window, which was now vibrating with the wind. "And put Sheriff Derek Connell in office, with his new right-hand man, Vickers."

Wolf caught the waitress's eye and waved for the check.

She came over, dropped the check and pulled the plate away.

Wolf smiled, avoiding eye contact as she left. "Thanks." It didn't matter that a beautiful woman was coming on to him; he couldn't stop thinking about Sarah.

Rachette seemed to read his mind. "How's Mark doing?"

"He's conscious. He'll make a full recovery."

Rachette nodded and palmed the table. "And finally."

Wolf raised his eyes.

"You going to be sheriff of this frickin' town or what?" Rachette slid out of the booth sideways.

CHAPTER 45

WOLF WAS grateful for the wind and rain outside on the day of his brother's funeral. He didn't need the visual of his brother being lowered next to his father anyway.

Instead the service had been held inside, and now that the sad affair was finally over, Wolf and his mother stood next to the chapel door giving hugs and gratitude to a dwindling line of family and friends. An icy breeze fluttered against them as another guest left and headed out into the fall storm.

Sarah lingered at the back of the line with folded arms, nodding for people to cut in front of her. Jack stood at his mother's side staring at Wolf with sad eyes, and Wolf winked with a reassuring smile.

Margaret Hitchens was next in line. Gripping Wolf's arms she said, "I'm so grateful you're okay, David. And I'm so sorry for what I allowed to happen with the council vote." She stared hard into his eyes, then nodded quickly. "We'll be appointing the right man for sheriff on Monday."

She reached up, kissed him on the cheek, and left.

With agonizing slowness, the line oozed out the door and Wolf was finally face to face with Sarah and Jack.

Sarah took a hug from his mother and accepted the barrage of compliments about her appearance, then turned to Wolf. "Can we talk?"

"Sure."

"Jack, give us a few minutes, okay?" Sarah said, grabbing Wolf's arm and tucking herself close as they passed through the door into the driving drizzle.

Looking back, Wolf caught Jack raising his eyebrows, a hopeful expression on his face that wrenched Wolf's gut.

They walked down the chapel steps towards the whipping blue tarp that covered his brother's grave.

"How is Mark doing?" He gave her a sidelong glance, trying to sound sincere.

She nodded, keeping her eyes on the ground. "He's doing great. He's sleeping a lot, but I've also been talking to him. He wakes up for a couple hours each day now."

"That's good, Sarah." Wolf gripped the umbrella with two hands as another gust hit.

Sarah squeezed the inside of his arm and shivered.

After a few more seconds of silence he asked, "What's going on, Sarah?"

She stared forward and took a deep breath, like she was psyching herself up. "I want to tell you about what happened. About how ... things fell apart. About everything. It can't wait any longer. And I'm so sorry I'm telling you today, on this day." She looked towards the graves of his brother and father, and her lips quivered as tears streamed down her face. She stopped and let go of his arm, and wiped her cheeks with both hands.

He stopped and turned to block the wind. "Just tell me."

She exhaled, then looked up at him with her sky-blue eyes. "When you went into the army, after your dad died, I was pregnant."

Wolf stared at her dumbly. "What? I don't understan—"

"Just let me talk, okay?"

Wolf nodded, "Okay."

She steeled her expression and spoke methodically. "And I had a miscarriage."

Wolf nodded again, and waited for her to continue speaking. With every moment she didn't continue speaking, Wolf felt his skin flush hotter and hotter.

"I don't understand," he said. "I ... why didn't you tell me? This was why you became hooked on drugs? Why we broke up? I don't understand."

"No, David, you don't understand," she looked at Wolf with a pleading expression.

"Then tell me." Wolf regretted his harsh tone immediately.

Her expression turned hard for an instant, then softened as she took another deep breath. "You came home two days after it happened. You came home from a mission. It was around my birthday. Do you remember? I was sick that week, and I didn't want to ... you know, get intimate."

Wolf did remember. "Yes. You were sick," he said quietly. "I had no idea."

"I hadn't yet told you about how I was pregnant. I hadn't even told my mom, and I was going to surprise you. I was going to surprise you when you came home." Her face stretched into a pained smile.

Wolf stepped forward to hold her, to comfort her.

She held up her hands. "Please, no. David, we have to talk about all of this. I have to get everything out."

He stopped and nodded dumbly.

"That week was when it all started. I had been so stressed out and just ... freaked out about being pregnant, but I didn't want to talk to you about it over the phone, from thousands of miles away. I didn't want to distract you from the danger you were facing every day. I knew you were coming home, and so I waited. And then it happened, just before you ..." She broke into new tears. "I thought I had caused it. I thought I had caused it because I was so stressed out, because I hadn't told you." The words were tumbling out of her now. "I should have told you. I caused it. It's my fault."

Wolf stepped forward and hugged her. "No you didn't. These things happen, Sarah. They happen to a lot of couples. It wasn't your fault. It happens."

She buried her face into his jacket and cried.

Wolf stroked her shoulder and stared into the sideways drizzle. Then he closed his eyes and relished the feeling of having Sarah close to him, of her finally opening up and letting her feelings show, for giving him a chance to comfort her, and giving him a chance to understand. There was such a rush of endorphins flowing through him that he was suddenly gripped with shame. He had just heard the most terrible news of his life, and yet he hadn't felt this ... good in years. This alive. This relieved.

She pulled back and wiped her eyes.

Wolf watched her as she pulled out a tissue and gently blew her nose, turning away to hide the act, and he thought that only she could make expelling mucus look cute.

"I was hooked on the painkillers after that week for over six months. Then I just stopped. Totally quit, cold-turkey. And then, three years later, we got married, and I got pregnant with Jack. And then something snapped inside after we had him." She sniffed. "I just ... kept thinking about the first baby, and how I had screwed it all up."

Wolf started for her again, and stopped when she held up her hands.

"And I think there was partly some post-partum depression, but I started taking the painkillers again. And then I started drinking. Then I took more painkillers, and drank more. I don't even remember most of that time. Don't remember being a mother." She shook her head. "I was a terrible mother. And one day, I was living with my parents, and they were taking care of Jack. And you were gone."

Wolf felt another wave of shame for being gone so much.

"And I was just so depressed. So I ..." She shrugged and flipped her hand. "Just kept going. Then my parents took over completely with Jack, and tried to help me, but at that point I'd gone overboard, as you know."

Wolf took a deep breath. He did know. He remembered the physical and mental transformation she'd gone through while he was in the army. It was startling to come home to a completely different person, one that was the complete opposite of the one he'd loved. It was one of the reasons, the many complicated reasons, he'd gotten out and started a new life at home in the department.

She stared at the ground for a while, then raised her head to Wolf with a determined look. "I'm through punishing myself." Her voice was resolute through clenched teeth. "I'm through punishing myself, and I'm through punishing everybody."

Wolf smiled gently and nodded. A gust of wind battered the umbrella and an icy spray of rain sucked the back of his suit pants to his legs.

Sarah stood silently, shifting her weight, like she had something else to say. She turned her head at the approach of pattering footfalls; it was Jack running toward them.

Sarah turned to Wolf. "David, Mark has asked me to move in with him." She looked up at him and crossed her arms against the cold.

Wolf raised his brow. "Ah." It was all he could think to say.

"And I've said yes."

Wolf felt the entire planet spin underneath him. "What?"

The thumping footfalls were on them now, and Jack slammed against Wolf's side, clutching him in a hug. "Jeez, it's freezing!" He kept his latch tight, burrowing the side of his face into Wolf's chest.

"What are you guys talking about?" Jack asked, looking between them.

Wolf watched Sarah look into the drizzle behind them.

"He-llo," Jack said. "What? Were you guys talking about me?"

Wolf pulled his arm out from Jack's clutches and patted his back.

"What were you guys talking about?" Jack asked again.

"Nothing." Wolf said, the chill of his voice matching the blustery air. "We were just saying good bye." He forced a smile and rubbed his son's head. "Good bye. I'll see you later."

"Okay. Later."

Sarah silently beckoned their son, turned, and walked away.

CHAPTER 46

Wolf walked out of the half-standing ranch house at the sound of approaching tires. A spotless black Audi, shining in the morning sun, rolled to a stop. Margaret Hitchens climbed out and walked fast around the rear bumper. She held a packet of fluttering papers in her hand between thumb and forefinger.

"Whatcha doing?" She looked to be suppressing a smile.

Wolf walked to his SUV and threw a duffle bag in the back seat. "Hi, Margaret. How are you?"

Her smile shone through. Putting the papers behind her back, she loped forward with long strides. "Where were you this morning?"

He shrugged. "Sleeping. I had a lot to catch up on."

She scoffed. "Well? Have you heard?"

"No," he lied. He'd already gotten a few harassing phone calls. "Heard what?"

"Congratulations." She thrust out her hand. "Sheriff Wolf."

He smiled without any teeth and shook her hand. "Thanks, Margaret."

She smirked. "You *have* already heard." She looked around, making a sour face at the pile of charred rubble that used to be the kitchen, then at the duffle bag on the seat. "Again, David, whatcha doing?"

He shut the SUV door. "Moving out. Actually, I'm going to need your help finding some place to rent."

"Yeah. That's kind of why I'm here. I want you to see something." She pulled the packet of paper in front of her and held it out.

Wolf took it.

A hyphenated-name of a law firm was printed in the top left of the front page, and the heading said, *Revocable Transfer on Death Deed.*

Wolf gave it back and walked towards the barn. "Just tell me. I'd rather save myself the embarrassment."

She slapped the papers on her leg and walked after him. "It shows the property we are standing on right now as transferrable to one *David Wolf* in the event of Gary Connell's death."

Wolf stopped and turned.

She held out the papers again.

Wolf walked slowly back and snatched the packet from her hand. It looked legitimate enough.

He gave her a sly squint. "How did you get this?"

She shrugged and sniffed. "What can I say? I have my sources."

"Huh."

She nodded. "Yeah."

Wolf's face scrunched and he looked again. "This just doesn't make any sense."

Or maybe it did.

Wolf flipped again through the pages while Margaret watched in silence.

Was Gary so fraught with regret about what he'd done sixteen years ago that he'd left Wolf the ranch in his will?

Or had Gary left Wolf the ranch as a ruse? An insurance policy, to make it seem like he'd cared about Wolf more than he had when Wolf was dead and gone?

It didn't matter.

He raised an eyebrow. "Free and clear?"

She nodded.

"The whole property? All three hundred acres?"

She raised her eyebrows and nodded again.

He sucked in the crisp fall air and looked at the golden aspens, then the green field beyond the driveway that terminated in the dense pine forest, then up to the snow-dusted thirteen-thousand-foot peaks in the west, and finally at the charred remains of the ailing house his father had built twenty-five years ago.

Then he nodded once. "Fuckin-A."

She laughed. "That's what I said."

THE END

Thank you so much for reading The Silversmith. I hope you enjoyed the story, and if you did, thank you for taking a few moments to leave a review. As an independent author, exposure is everything, and positive reviews help so much to get that exposure. If you chose to leave an honest word about the book, I'd be so appreciative.

PLEASE LEAVE A REVIEW HERE

I love interacting with readers so please feel free to email me at jeff@jeffcarson.co so I can thank you personally. Otherwise, thank you very much for your support by other means, such as sharing the books with your friends/family/book clubs/the weird guy who wears tight women's yoga pants at the coffee shop, or anyone else you think might be interested in reading the David Wolf books. Thanks again and I hope to see you again inside another Wolf story.

Would you like to know about future David Wolf books the moment they are published? You can visit my blog and sign up for the New Release Newsletter at this link -- http://www.jeffcarson.co/p/newsletter.html

As a gift for signing up you'll receive a complimentary copy of Gut Decision—A David Wolf Short Story, which is a harrowing tale that takes place years ago during David Wolf's first days in the Sluice County Sheriff's Department.

Gut Decision (A David Wolf Short Story)– Sign up for the new
release newsletter at http://www.jeffcarson.co/p/
newsletter.html and receive a complimentary copy.

PREVIEW OF ALIVE AND KILLING
(DAVID WOLF BOOK 3)

"MY DAD and I used to hike up there a lot. I love it up there ..."

And there was number four.

Wolf went back to blocking out the drone of the greasy-headed underachiever in front of him and stared up at a spider web in the corner of the ceiling. It was high up, gently swaying on the breeze of the air-conditioner vent. Too high to stretch up and swipe it away, even with Wolf's six-foot-three reach.

At least Wolf liked that about his new office. The politics? The fact that he had to be interviewing this candidate? *Those* were things he didn't like about his new office—his new position. But the ceilings? He loved the airy and light feel of the tall space.

He could probably scoot a chair underneath it and get at it. Wolf blew a puff of air out of his nose as he realized how much thought he was putting into the whole thing.

"Sheriff Wolf?"

Wolf snapped back to attention and looked at the interviewee.

He was smiling at Wolf, like he wanted in on the joke. He looked to the corner of the ceiling. "Whoa, got a doozy of a web up there. Don't they clean this place?" He laughed too loud and sat back with one arm hooked to the back of the chair. Then he wiped his nose with a sniff and crossed his leg, displaying a smudge of dirt on the knee of his jeans. The sudden movement pushed another wave of body odor across Wolf's desk.

Nineteen-year-old Kevin Ash, son of the new chairman of the town council of Rocky Points, Charlie Ash, was a shoo-out, and Wolf had just about heard and seen enough.

The only points Wolf could give the kid on self-presentation were for the collared shirt. Unfortunately, it looked like he'd been storing the shirt in a tennis-ball can for the past year, and demerits for ill-fitting jeans and beyond-broken-in muddy hiking boots negated said points.

Kevin winked conspiratorially. "I'll tell my dad they need to get someone on that."

Then there were the shameless mentions of his father in order to help his chances of getting hired. That was *the fifth.* And that was enough.

Wolf stood up and held out his hand. "Thanks, Kevin. I've got your résumé, and I'll be in touch."

A confident smile stretched across Kevin's face as he stood.

Wolf shook his hand, walked around his desk, and pushed him gently toward the door. He opened it, and pushed him a little harder into the hall.

"Uh, I guess I'll check in with my father, or whatever, or I'll just wait and see—"

"Yeah, don't worry. I'll be telling your father what I think. I'll definitely be in touch with him."

Relief replaced worry on Kevin's face and he strutted his way through the squad room in front of Wolf. Kevin nodded and slapped his hand on the corner of Deputy Baine's desk on the way by.

Baine raised an eyebrow and looked up from his paperwork.

208 / JEFF CARSON

Wolf walked Kevin Ash through the door into and through reception, and then propped open the outside door with one hand. He waved Kevin out, sending him into the cool early June morning, and out of his life.

"Thank you so much, Sheriff W—"

The door clicked shut and Wolf walked to the glass-enclosed reception desk where Tammy Granger sat glaring.

"Tammy. If you let another—"

Tammy coughed loud, pointing a discreet finger toward the seating area behind Wolf.

Wolf glanced behind him and saw a woman in her early twenties sitting stiffly, gaze fixed straight ahead out the window. Wolf noticed that her feet weren't touching the ground, and estimated her at no more than five-foot two-inches tall. Unlike Kevin Ash, she wore business casual, dressed in dark slacks and jacket.

She turned to him and smiled with a curt nod, a gesture that portrayed confidence and poise, and then went back to staring outside, looking like she was doing a particularly tough calculation in her head, and solving it.

Wolf turned back to Tammy and gave another glance over his shoulder, intrigued by the interaction.

He caught Tammy's scowl and felt his face flush. He shouldn't have kicked Kevin Ash out of the building like he had. But the process of hiring a new deputy was getting to him, and the presence of Ash's son was a flick in the ear he hadn't needed from the council chairman. It was one thing that they were pushing him with an unreasonable deadline to choose a new deputy to hire; it was quite another to force him to look at candidates like Kevin Ash—complete wastes of his time.

Wolf leaned a forearm on the reception counter and raised an eyebrow.

Tammy kept a blank face and scooted a manila folder across.

He didn't grab it, and kept staring. She wasn't giving any tells. Wolf shook his head. He liked Tammy. She was the forebrain of the department, manning the phones and any walk-ins, and she was also a motherly presence. She looked out for all the deputies, keeping abreast of their personal lives, so as to make sure they were living right. If a deputy came in hung over, she'd know about it, and browbeat said deputy into promising better behavior in the future. If a deputy had wronged a spouse, or a town member, they would have Tammy to answer to when she heard about it through the grapevine.

At two hundred pounds, she was built like a mountain woman who'd spent as much time cooking as chopping wood to heat the fires she cooked with. She was imposing, but smart, and also compassionate. In Wolf's estimation, it was a combination that made her one of the best employees in the entire department. He likened her to a worthy assistant football coach.

And since Wolf was the head coach now, having been sheriff for a little over eight months, he valued his assistant coach's opinion. Wolf knew she had an opinion of the candidate sitting behind him. Tammy had studied the applications harder than he had, and the all-important first-impression rating was in the books, no doubt supporting what she had gleaned from the résumé.

True to form, she wasn't letting on anything. Maybe Tammy was too disappointed in the entire process to play the game. They both knew that the woman sitting in the lobby was Wolf's final interview, and then time was up.

He needed to choose a new deputy by Thursday, in two days, or the money would not be coming from the state of Colorado. The Sluice County Council had made it clear to

Wolf—they needed that money. Either he made a choice, or they would make it for him.

As the days of Gary Connell, the deceased former council chairman, and his bottomless pockets receded in the rearview mirror, the council's money-grabbing was beginning to take on the personality of a hungry bear. They were ripping through the county, and the town of Rocky Points, upturning every opportunity to get any sort of funding, every cent from every source.

First they had concocted the idea of the Rocky Points Music Festival, which was taking place this weekend, kicking off Friday, and now there was the new hire.

It was clear to everyone that Wolf and his deputies were being proactive, and were ready for the upcoming music festival. But as far as the new hire went, the council thought Wolf was dragging his feet. He wasn't. He just wasn't going to hire some lackey to fill a quota. And he wasn't going to hire Kevin Ash, the new council chairman's moronic son just to fill the position and to score some political points.

However, and what Tammy knew just as well as Wolf, the seven candidates he'd seen so far had fallen woefully short. And, now, here was the final contender. She was also a "recommendation" by a council member, Margaret Hitchens.

Chairman Ash's nepotistic hopes were certainly going to be denied by Wolf. If he had to disappoint two council members—well, that was probably going to make things sticky for his future.

Wolf took a breath and slapped the manila folder on his leg, and then turned with a smile. "Heather Patterson?"

She scooted forward until her feet were flat on the ground, and then stood up and faced Wolf. "Yes, sir."

Wolf was startled by her short stature, and he knew he was showing it.

Her glacial pool-blue eyes were unwavering as she stepped

forward with an outstretched hand. Her shoulder-length dark-brown hair had a tint of auburn in it, and it was pulled back on one side, fastened with a series of silver hair clips.

Her handshake grip was small, firm, and confident, like the rest of her seemed to be.

"Nice to meet you," Wolf said.

"Likewise."

Wolf waved a hand toward the door. "This way."

She stepped past Wolf, wafting a soft, flowery aroma into his nostrils. The smell of Kevin Ash was finally a memory.

The door clicked and they entered the squad room.

Click here to get Alive and Killing (A David Wolf Novel) and continue reading Wolf's next adventure ...

This has been a work of fiction. Names, characters, businesses, places, events, and incidents are either the products of the

Made in the USA
Las Vegas, NV
15 July 2023

74775907R00127